The shower door opened slowly...

Jack watched as Perry stood there, naked and dripping. Her hair hung in wet hanks to the tops of her breasts. It was jet-black, the same color as her big bright eyes.

Her skin on the other hand was lily-white, a delicate porcelain pale, the only color that of the dark cherry centers of her breasts. He'd tasted her, made love to her, had her mouth on him, but there was something about seeing her like this that wound him up hot and tight.

"I want to know something," she said, backing up when he started toward her.

He climbed into the shower, breathing deeply of the spice and the steam. "What's that?"

"The case. What are you going to do next?"

It was hard to take her interest in his business seriously when they were both wet and naked. Jack sighed. "Don't do this, Perry."

"Don't do what?"

"Get involved with me...make this into something it's not."

She paused. "Then tell me, Jack. What is going on here?"

"It's just sex, Perry. That's all."

Yet they both knew that was a lie.

Blaze™

Dear Reader,

I hope you've read the special Blaze anthology
Red Letter Nights (Nov. 2005), and the follow-up book by
the fabulous Karen Anders, *Give Me Fever* (Dec. 2005).
In February 2006 watch for another sexy story in our
New Orleans–set series, *Going All Out,* this one by the
talented Jeanie London.

This month, however, I'm pleased to bring you the story
of Jack Montgomery and Perry Brazille. Perry you met in
my *Red Letter Nights* novella, "Luv U Madly." And Jack first
came onto the scene as the bass player for "the deck" in
my 1999 Harlequin Temptation novel, *Four Men & a Lady.*

The reunion story's opening chapters found Jack onstage
fronting for his band, Diamond Jack. Later, at the picnic
and ball game, he talked about his days in military service,
about seeing enough of the world. Well, this is where I
finally learned more about what Jack had seen and where
he'd been. I also discovered what he'd done and what he'd
suffered.

Goes Down Easy is the story of two people for whom no
other love exists. It also wraps up the tales of the final
three of my original four men. I hope you enjoy Jack's
adventure and the great romance he shares with his very
own Gypsy woman, Perry Brazille. Please visit my
Web site at www.alisonkent.com to learn more about
what I'm now writing for my favorite line in the world—
Harlequin Blaze.

Alison Kent

GOES DOWN EASY
Alison Kent

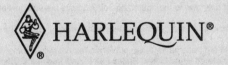

HARLEQUIN®

TORONTO • NEW YORK • LONDON
AMSTERDAM • PARIS • SYDNEY • HAMBURG
STOCKHOLM • ATHENS • TOKYO • MILAN • MADRID
PRAGUE • WARSAW • BUDAPEST • AUCKLAND

This one is for the readers whose letters keep me going and whose daily visits
to my blog help keep my feet on the ground and my head out of the clouds.
You all are the best.

A special acknowledgment goes to Laurie Damron, who graciously took the
time to read this story in its initial incarnation and helped me make it better.

Also, thank you to Colleen Collins and Shaun Kauffman for answering my
question about P.I. legalities. Any and all gaffes are my own.

ISBN 0-373-79229-8

GOES DOWN EASY

This edition published by arrangement with Harlequin Books S.A.

® and TM are trademarks of the publisher. Trademarks indicated with
® are registered in the United States Patent and Trademark Office, the
Canadian Trade Marks Office and in other countries.

www.eHarlequin.com

Printed in U.S.A.

1

THE TRAIL went cold in New Orleans the same time as the weather, a double header for which Jack Montgomery wasn't prepared. Since hired by Cindy Eckhardt to look into the kidnapping of her husband Dayton—chief executive for Eckton Computing and missing since New Year's Day—he'd reveled in all kinds of heat.

First there was the temperature that had the Gulf Coast in an unseasonably sweaty grip. Next, the series of hot leads that had him hoofin' it across the state line, from Texas into Louisiana. Finally, the burning in his gut that made him believe this case was going to go down like cream.

But then the tables had turned, flipping him a big fat bird. And now he found himself standing in the middle of Jackson Square, a week into the new year, freezing his ass off and wondering whether he'd be doing better to turn left or right.

It wasn't that Cindy, the trophy wife nearly thirty years her husband's junior, didn't trust the cops or the feds to get the job done, as much as it was her needing to know someone had her back. Especially since

Dayton's heart medication had been found on the ground at the kidnapping scene, and a week into the case the authorities were no closer to a solution than they'd been on day one.

He started walking aimlessly. The sign for Café Eros came into view, reminding him that he was hungry enough to eat a six-foot submarine sandwich. Café Eros, eh? Well, he'd never been one to turn his back on love—even if right now the only affair he was interested in involved his stomach and a whole lot of food.

Burrowing into his hooded sweatshirt, Jack headed for the building's courtyard. He jogged up the stairs to the small eatery's second floor, hoping it wasn't busy, not in the mood for a crowd.

Too much noise interfered with his ability to process information, to analyze, to reason, to think—which was why he and special ops had made such a good fit for eight of his twelve years in the Marines. The missions he had run required secrecy, and communication was often accomplished with hand signals and nothing more.

When hitting a dead end like this one, however, he doubted even total silence would help. What he needed was a sign. But first he needed a sandwich.

At the counter, behind which was painted a mural of a swaggering swashbuckler, Jack ordered a bowl of gumbo and half a muffuletta. When in Rome, and all that. He took a seat at a table decorated with a purple, green and gold Mardi Gras tablecloth and picked up a copy of the *Times-Picayune*.

He scanned the front page, listening to the smoky jazz playing from the café's corner speakers—God, he loved jazz—sipping at a hot chicory coffee blend, the warmth of the mug thawing his fingers and doing a good job of heating up the iceberg in his gut. He was not cut out for the cold.

He'd lived most of his life in Texas for that very reason. His three tours of duty were the only years he'd spent away from the Lone Star State. Bring on the heat and humidity; that was his motto. Even the mosquitoes and the ragweed couldn't drive him away.

Nothing in his life had prepared him for what he'd suffered during his years in special ops—the lack of food, of sleep, of shelter, often of contact with another soul whose native tongue was the same as his. And weather so hot and humid, the air so heavy with moisture that there were days that just breathing had been hard work.

Ending his trip down weather lane, he turned to page two, eating as he skimmed the paper. The coffee was hot and biting, the gumbo steaming with spicy sausage and the tang of tomatoes, okra and bay leaf. At this rate he might dig in and stay for awhile.

Sounded a lot more appealing than admitting he'd screwed up somewhere, and that the job he'd taken at the request of the Eckhardt family was quickly heading down the tubes. He'd been surprised when Becca Nelson, the University of Texas coed who ran his Austin-based private investigation business between classes from her Blackberry, had told him of Cindy Eckhardt's call.

He had a reputation for finding people who didn't want to be found. The sixteen-year-old Dallas trust funder who'd wanted to play in a rock 'n' roll band. The bride from Fort Worth who'd changed her mind on the way to the church. Most recently, the San Antonio bank executive who'd left his position in the midst of a midlife crisis, taking a new name—and a whole lot of his employer's money with him.

Jack owed much of the notoriety to Becca. She was in the fifth year of her four-year degree plan, having spent thirty-six months working her way around the world before starting school at twenty-one. Since hiring on five years ago when he'd first set up shop, answering an ad he'd placed in the UT newspaper the *Daily Texan*, she'd made it her mission to get his name out there in an effort to ensure job security.

Hers.

She'd had no problem with the fact that he ran his business out of his SUV, and had taken over converting him to a rolling electronic wonder, crawling around with a tool belt bigger than she was, outfitting the Yukon's dashboard to resemble a Black Hawk cockpit.

She'd set up the meeting with the Eckhardt family, flooded his PDA with scanned clippings and e-mailed him online stories. Seemed Cindy and Dayton had been loading the car New Year's morning, heading for the airport and an Aspen vacation, when the kidnapping went down.

With Dayton outside, Cindy had made one last trip into their Hyde Park home, coming out less than ten minutes later to find Dayton gone, the doors of his Lexus wide open, suitcases strewn about.

The police had taken one look at the obvious signs of a struggle, interviewed witnesses who'd seen two masked men in a black Jeep without plates and put out an APB.

Enough of the crime's details had been in the news that Jack wasn't surprised things had begun going south. The kidnappers had only to flip on a local broadcast and hear everything the media proclaimed the public had a right to know.

Screw that. Dayton Eckhardt wasn't the public's husband or father. No one but the Eckhardt family, the Austin PD and the FBI had a right to anything. And, the way he saw it, in that order—the very reason he checked in with Cindy every few hours, new news or not.

Unfortunately, so many of the particulars had been leaked that the kidnappers were no longer even a blip on the radar. If anything, they were burrowed deep underground. Three days and counting, the police were down to zero leads and were *still* waiting for a ransom demand. Jack had lucked out with the New Orleans connection—especially since the feds had turned up nothing much in Louisiana beyond rumors that a psychic was involved.

Dayton Eckhardt had started Eckton Computing in the Big Easy before market conditions—property taxes, salaries, the value of a square foot of warehouse space—had sent the start-up to Austin a year ago. Eckhardt had left behind more than a few disgruntled employees—not to mention, rumor had it, Dayton's disgruntled mistress.

One of the ex-employees Jack had interviewed thought she'd seen Dayton at a Christmas party in the Quarter. That made no sense, but it was the only scrap Jack had, and he held on tight. There had been no activity on Dayton's cell phone since the kidnapping, and none on his personal or corporate e-mail accounts. At least nothing outgoing. There had been plenty of incoming, and most of it junk. Even that had been analyzed by the Eckton tech working with the Austin PD. So far, nothing but ads for erectile dysfunction meds and spam mail promising live sex via webcams.

Jack was more into having fun with the real thing. Or he would be, one of these days. When he found the time. When he found the woman. When he found a reason to look for either instead of spending his time looking for strangers who'd vanished without a trace. Instead of looking to find himself.

His life had been in flux for a while, the transition from special ops to civilian PI tougher than he'd anticipated. Six years ago at his fifteenth high school reunion, after catching up with his friends who'd made up "the deck"—he'd been the jack, Quentin the queen, Heidi the joker, Ben the ace, Randy the king—fitting back into real life had seemed a doable prospect.

The three-day reunion had been a hell of a party. He'd stood onstage at The Cave Down Below—the warehouse club booked for that Friday night—looked out at the four friends who'd been his high school anchors and choked himself up, barely recovering before belting out Bruce Springsteen's "Born in the USA."

He remembered sitting on a picnic table next to Heidi the next day, and telling her about not wanting to hit eighty and wonder how he got there. Or what happened during the years in between.

And even though he'd been tired of traveling the world, he hadn't been quite ready to settle down. He'd continued to drift for a couple of years after the reunion, living on the road and out of his duffel bag for the full tour that he'd fronted for Diamond Jack, the band he'd put together once his discharge had come through.

Music had been a huge part of his life for as long as he could remember. His days playing bass in "the deck's" high school ensemble had been one of the best times of his life. He'd learned about belonging. About true friendships and human nature, about faults and flaws and royally freaking things up—which was exactly what he'd done after graduation.

And here he'd gone and done the same thing now. *No, dude. You didn't. You're just stuck with the big stinkin' pile of crap left by everyone who worked this case before you.* Telling himself that was a whole lot easier than buying it as the truth.

Truth held position number one at the top of Jack's culpability barometer. And not the ask-me-no-questions-and-I'll-tell-you-no-lies sort of honesty he'd witnessed too often, but balls-to-the-wall-or-die.

If knowledge was power, then truth was omnipotence…and was why Jack nearly sputtered gumbo across the newspaper when he flipped to page fifteen, and the headline halfway down leaped out.

Psychic Della Brazille to consult on Eckhardt kidnapping

What the hell?

Oh no. This wasn't happening. He wasn't having his case all mucked up by a scammer out to fleece a family already on the edge. After the hurt he'd seen during his years in special ops, the anger, the pain—and having to learn to live with it all—there was no way he'd let anyone latch on like a leech to his case.

Especially not a con artist more interested in fifteen minutes of fame than anything resembling reality—or truth.

PERRY BRAZILLE GROANED at the headline, thankful the story had been buried on page fifteen rather than splashed across page one. Della so did not need to see this newest mention connecting her to the case. The stress she was under was already making her sick.

She'd been bombarded by the media, by former employees of Eckton Computing, by the Eckhardt family—all of them seeking answers she didn't have to give. But the biggest stress came from the visions themselves. Visions which had started weeks ago and plagued her ever since.

That was how it had been with Della from the beginning, Perry mused, hiking up her calf-length skirt's yards of navy twill and climbing onto the stool behind the counter in Sugar Blues. Her aunt never saw things in her dreams, or as gentle imaginings.

What she saw instead came as flashes. Harsh and jolting. Migraine-inducing. Blasts of intense color and heat and dizzying sound, each flash more draining, more agonizing than the last. It was an affliction which she'd suffered all of her life.

Della was, in fact, upstairs sleeping after hours of excruciating pain. And Perry intended to see that her aunt—her last living relative, the woman who, though only eighteen years older, had been Perry's mother for most of her life—slept as long as she needed to.

That was why she was at the shop's counter now. Della had three appointments for evening readings that needed to be rescheduled. Two were with old clients who would hate the delay but, being devoted to Della, would totally understand.

The third appointment was with Claire Braden who was new to Sugar Blues and the world of psychic readings. Claire was one of Perry's neighbors at Court du Chaud. The "hot" court had been christened as such when occupied by Captain Gabriel Dampier, now the resident ghost.

Longtime occupants of Court du Chaud were well-versed in the legend of the pirate and his band. Perry had never seen him herself, but both Tally and Bree Addison, the twins living in numbers one and one-and-a-half, had shared stories of their sightings.

Perry's experience was with a ghost of a different color—a blues singer named Sugar Babin who'd fallen (some said been pushed) to her death down the stairs of the very building that served as Della's place of business, and had been her home for all of her life. It had been Perry's, too, for many years.

At least Sugar only haunted the stairwell between the bottom step and the top, singing of love gone wrong in her smoky Nina Simone-like voice. And here Perry had always hoped there would be no PMS in the afterlife.

She dialed Claire's office number, and when the other woman picked up, said, "Hey, it's me. Della's not feeling well, so I'm going to have to reschedule you, okay?"

"Of course it's okay. Wait, no. Don't reschedule. Just cancel. This reading was all your idea anyway, remember?"

Using the appointment book's pen with the cobalt blue feather, Perry drew a line of tiny X's through Claire's name, thinking of another of their Court du Chaud neighbors, Tally Addison, who'd recently come to Sugar Blues seeking help. "It was a suggestion, not an ultimatum. Tally left after her visit with her mind more at ease. I thought Della might do the same for you."

"Tally's problems were with Court du Chaud's ghost, not a man who wants to elope instead of spending money on a wedding." Claire was obviously still arguing with her fiancé of one month about their upcoming spring nuptials.

"Randy still being a cheapskate?" A funny turn of events, considering the way he'd tossed money around before meeting Claire.

"I only plan to get married once in my life. I'd like the full designer gown, doves, balloons and ribbons package, ya know?" Claire sighed. "I think I liked Randy better when he believed money *could* buy happiness."

"No, you didn't. You just happened to be in the driver's seat then. Now he's keeping you on your toes." Though Perry was quite sure that Claire's toes were the last body part Randy had on his mind.

Claire's sigh filled the void in the conversation. "I suppose he's worth it."

"Oh, stop it already," Perry said, drawing little O's above the X's. "You know he is, and if you don't, well, send him my way."

"No can do, girlfriend. He bakes me cookies." Claire laughed as if nothing more needed to be said.

And Perry supposed nothing did. She didn't know a single female who wouldn't dig on having a man with culinary skills that went beyond throwing burgers on a grill and popping the top on a beer can.

She certainly would, though she didn't see it happening since her life had always revolved around women. A choice she'd made too many years ago to count. "I've still got room in my freezer if you have more you need to unload. Never can unload too many cookies, you know. At least from a calorie/wedding dress perspective."

Claire laughed a second time. "See? Eloping would get me out of that worry. I could wear blue jeans, and all would be right with the world."

"Wait. Back up," Perry said as the bell over the

shop's front door chimed. She glanced up to see a man shove back the hood of his navy hoodie before disappearing into the shop's aisles. "I thought you didn't want to elope. That you wanted to know what Della could tell you about your wedding."

"I did, but I've changed my mind."

"Fickle, much?" Perry asked, straightening on the stool to peek over the bookcase that ran like a divider down the center of the shop. She saw brown hair flecked with bits of blond and a touch of gray at the man's temples. She also saw long, long, *long* lashes that made her want to cry with envy.

"Probably less than it seems," Claire was saying.

"How so?"

"Well, for example, if I were to have a baby, I wouldn't want to know its sex in advance."

"Hmm," Perry said, more interested in her customer than in Claire's attempt at logic. If only the stupid bookshelf were five instead of six feet tall. "Are you and Randy already talking about kids?"

"Please! It's way too soon for that. We're still learning what we can about each other."

"Besides your shared cookie fetish?"

Claire groaned. "I swear. I'm going to be an elephant before we ever set a date."

"Maybe, but Randy's a good guy." Perry smiled to herself, returning the plumed pen to its base. "He'll be there through thin and through thick."

"Ha! A comedian in every crowd."

"I was raised by a woman who sees things she shouldn't be able to see. I have to get my laughs somewhere."

"God, Perry. I can't even imagine a lifetime of dealing with that. I would think it would be so…I don't know. Frightening?"

Perry shoved a hand through her hair, pushing the wild corkscrew curls away from her face. She had never talked to anyone about growing up with Della, about Della having to deal with the truth of her visions. Having to deal as well with both of their fears that the aftermath might one day debilitate her, leaving Perry alone again and too young to cope. Frightening was only a part of it.

"That. And interesting." To say the least, which was all she could say for now. "I've gotta run. Are you sure you want to cancel?"

"Definitely," Claire said, and Perry could almost hear the other woman nod. "But let's do dinner one night this week."

"Cookies for dessert?"

"What else?" Claire asked, laughing and adding, "I'll call you," before ringing off.

Once she had, Perry was left with no reason to stay at the counter. And even if she'd had tons of work to do there, curiosity would still have gotten the better of her. It wasn't every day a man who looked like the one an aisle over walked into the shop.

She climbed down from the stool, closed the leather appointment book and stored it on end next to the cash register she locked out of habit. Then, smoothing down her skirt and the hem of her paisley-print poet's blouse, she hooked the key ring on her index finger and went to check him out.

He was well worth checking out. The hint of gray had fooled her from a distance; he was no older than his late thirties, she guessed. He wore jeans and Reeboks with his hoodie. The neckband of a white T-shirt showed above the eyelets where the drawstrings hung loose.

He stood studying a display of ground marble and resin figurines representing the twelve astrological signs, designed by a local artisan. He held a Taurus bull in one hand, an Aries ram in the other. Perry wondered if she should read anything into his selections or just let it go.

She nodded toward the figurines. "Those are one of our most popular items. The artist has made quite a name for herself here. A true hometown success story."

He didn't glance up right away. Instead, he silently returned both items to the antique cherry cabinet. Then he turned and stared down at Perry until she was certain she would never again be able to breathe—she who had never been susceptible to the buff and chiseled type.

His eyes were gray, a dark pewter with silver specks. Up close, his lashes appeared even longer than they had from a distance. His eyes were amazing, gorgeous—as was his denim-and-cotton-covered build—but his expression scared her to death.

"May I help you?" she asked when the silence had gone on for too long.

"Della Brazille?"

Uh-oh. "Who's inquiring?"

"Me. And I'm here to make sure you keep your hocus-pocus fingers out of the Eckhardt kidnapping."

RED AND BLACK. Welts and bruises. Cuts and scrapes and raw purple skin. An arm. A hand. A missing finger.

The ring. It should be there. A class ring. A sports ring. Heavy and gold. It had been there before.

The watch remained. Platinum links. Multiple dials. The edge of a sleeve.

Torn, not cut, and stained with a rust color that had once been blood. Nothing more. Nothing else.

Only slices of light, crosshatched shadows, herringbone in yellow and blue. And so much watery, fluid green.

Della opened her eyes and sat up, pulling the bed's periwinkle chenille coverlet to her chin. She blinked slowly and let out a breath of relief. The pain was gone. She felt empty, spent…strangely weak and fragile.

Forty-eight years old and she ached like an ancient crone. It was enough to make her laugh. Except laughing would expend energy she didn't have to spare.

She scooted to the side of the bed, tugged down the hem of her fine lawn nightgown, and sat with her legs dangling over the edge of the mattress while picking up the bedside phone and dialing the NOPD.

"Operations."

"Detective Franklin, please." She waited thirty seconds before he came on the line.

"Franklin."

"Book. It's Della," she said, and hurried on. "They've cut off his finger. He was wearing a ring. A college bowl ring maybe? I can't say." She tucked the coverlet tighter. "I can only see the shape. The edge of the insignia."

"I'll be there in twenty minutes."

"He's still wearing a watch. And I think I see ropes."

"Della." Book's voice was firm, caring. "Hang on to it. I'm on my way."

2

"EXCUSE ME?"

Jack was pretty damn sure he hadn't stuttered. But just to be certain…

He pulled from his back pocket the newspaper he'd folded to the headline and dared her to deny her meddlesome ways. "The case is my business, got it? My business. Not yours."

She didn't even glance at the paper. She crossed her arms over her chest. She said nothing.

She was an intriguing little thing. Looked a lot like a gypsy. Black curls hanging in a cloud around a heart-shaped face. Big dark eyes and a bow of a mouth that meant business. About five foot eight—though the way she was staring him down, he wouldn't be surprised if she thought herself ten feet tall.

"Well?" he finally asked. She'd obviously gone mute.

"Well what?" Her eyes flashed.

A reaction, though not much of one. He'd have preferred an admission or a denial. Either one would make it easier to gauge his next step. "Are you going to back off or not?"

"Let's see." She held up one finger after another,

counting off her list. "You've been sarcastic, rude, demanding. You've come into my place of business and ordered me around, not even bothering to tell me who you are. And you want *me* to back off?"

Hands now at her hips, she shook her head, summing up the situation with a loud snort and an even louder, "Get the hell out of here."

Jack sighed, rubbed a hand over his forehead where the ache that had started three days ago in Austin remained.

"My name is Jack Montgomery," he said, returning the newspaper to his pocket and pulling out his wallet. He showed the woman his driver's license and identification card. "I'm a private investigator."

She barely even glanced at his ID. "Good for you. But you're in the Big Easy now, *cher*. Those won't even get you a bowl of gumbo."

His Texas card. Stupid. His Louisiana paperwork was in his computer case out in his Yukon, but she didn't give him time to explain. She turned and started to walk away. He didn't even think.

He reached out and grabbed her upper arm. "Della, wait."

She jerked free, glared over her shoulder. "I'm not Della."

What?

"I'm Della."

At the sound of the second female voice, deeper, almost musical, Jack looked up. Standing behind the shop's counter at the foot of the staircase that opened there, stood the most stunning woman he'd ever seen.

She was older than the one he'd mistaken her for, but he doubted she'd yet reached fifty. She was slender and barefoot, dressed in what looked like silk pajamas in gold and black. Her hair, a dark honey brown, had been pulled up into a knot already tumbling loose.

Her skin was a translucent porcelain, and he was so glad he wasn't saying any of this out loud because he sounded as fruity as one of the *Queer Eye* TV guys. Or so he imagined, since he'd never seen their show.

More than anything, though, he found himself caught by and unable to look away from her eyes. They were large, the irises purple, her expression serene even while he swore her stare was scrambling his brain like so many bad eggs.

"She does that to everyone."

He blinked, looked back at the gypsy. "What?"

"Della is my aunt, and you're not the first man she's turned into a drooling fool."

"I'm not drooling," he said, swiping the cuff of his sweatshirt over his chin.

"Perry, Book is on his way over," Della said, heading toward a beaded curtain hiding a door at the rear of the shop. "I'm making brunch. Spinach omelets, I think. Bring your friend."

The beads gave off a tinkling singsong sound as they settled. Neverland. No. La-la land. That's where he was. The funny farm. *Where life was beautiful...*

"Are you coming?"

This from the same woman—Perry—who'd ordered him off the property minutes before. "I thought you wanted me out of here."

She twisted her mouth as if she couldn't decide between smiling and snapping. Like a turtle. Clamping down on his nose and tearing it right off his face. "I do. But obviously Della doesn't."

"And she always gets her way?" He'd seen her. He didn't doubt for a minute that she did.

"You'll be able to figure that out for yourself soon enough."

It was exactly what he wanted—personal access, an *in*—yet he couldn't make himself take the first step. He'd been battling strange feelings about the case since taking it on.

And these two women weren't doing a damn thing to settle the uncertainty. They were, in fact, making things worse.

Making things…weird.

Perry took a step toward the door through which Della had disappeared, holding aside the strands of blue beads. "C'mon. You don't want to miss Della's omelets. And I know you're not going to want to miss comparing notes with Book."

Jack tensed at the twist of the be-careful-what-you-wish-for screw. "Who's Book?"

"He's a detective with the NOPD." Perry gave the screw one last tightening turn. "And he believes every word Della says to be the truth."

DETECTIVE BOOK FRANKLIN parked his unmarked car in the alley where a small courtyard backed up to Sugar Blues. He'd met Della Brazille right here two years ago, and nothing about his life had been the same.

He didn't know anyone who was a bigger skeptic or cynic than he was, and so he had a hard time explaining to his co-workers—he didn't have anyone outside the force he called a friend; he'd tried, but nobody understood a cop's hours and drive but another cop—why he jumped when Della called.

He shouldn't have jumped. He shouldn't have believed in her sight, or believed her visions meant anything, that they were more than nightmares or a fertile imagination seeking attention.

He lived in New Orleans. He'd run into plenty of psychics fitting that bill.

Straightening his tie as he made for the kitchen door, Book couldn't help remembering the first time he'd seen her here at the back entrance to Sugar Blues. There'd been a break-in and murder in the next building over, the security there no better than here.

She'd been sitting on the wall of the central fountain, soaking wet, wearing a silky camisole and thin drawstring pants. No shoes, nothing beneath. As if she'd pulled on the clothes without thinking of anything but what she'd seen. Hell, she might as well have been naked, wearing clothing that was plastered to her skin with the temperature in the forties.

When she'd told him about it, he'd thought she was relating details of a dream. Or that she'd been stoned out of her mind and tripping.

Perry had arrived minutes later, bundled her aunt up and, in the kitchen over hot coffee for him and herbal tea for both women, had explained Della's gift of sight.

He'd taken careful notes, still doubting he was doing more than recording a bunch of BS.

But the BS has paid off. Della had seen specifics about the perps' flight and spree that had followed. It had been enough for Book and his partner to use in their ongoing investigation. It had been enough to help them eventually nail the bastards' theft ring.

It had been enough to make Book believe.

That didn't mean he wasn't going to have a certain reporter's throat once he was finished here. Della's work on the Eckhardt kidnapping wasn't yet public because there wasn't yet an official case. Not in New Orleans anyway. She wasn't even positive it was Eckhardt.

She'd come to him with what she'd seen, and he'd taken the information and made the Texas connection himself. No one else in operations should have known about his inquiry. Meaning, Book had a big, fat internal leak to patch.

He knocked; through the inset glass he saw Perry wave him inside. He pushed open the door without even turning the knob, a knot forming in his stomach.

"I thought you were getting that fixed." As independent and intelligent as they were, the Brazille women were not so good with down-to-earth priorities. He'd get someone over here later today.

"Good morning, Book. I hope you're hungry."

At the sound of Della's voice, he turned, his attention shifting away from Perry and the door. Della stood grating cheese, her back to the room. Beside her, a man Book had never seen before leaned against the counter.

Perry made the introductions. "Detective Book Franklin? Jack Montgomery, private eye."

Cripes. And the day just kept going downhill.

He shook the hand Montgomery offered—a firm grip that went on seconds too long as the other man took Book's measure. He did the same. Neither spoke, and it was Perry who finally ended the standoff with a muttered, "Oh, good grief."

At that, Della laughed and glanced over. "Jack is here for the same reason you are, Book."

He cursed beneath his breath. "I was hoping you hadn't seen the paper."

"She hasn't," Perry hurried to say.

"Of course I have." Della sealed up the block of cheese in its container and handed it to Jack. "And, no," she added as he returned the cheese to the fridge. "Jack didn't show it to me. It was part of what I saw this morning before I called."

"You *saw* the headline. But not the actual paper."

Della nodded at Montgomery's rhetorical statement. Book shoved his hands to his waist, his coattails flying like bat wings behind him, instead of grabbing the other man and tossing him out on his ear. "Perry, do you mind giving me a few minutes alone with Della?"

"Sure. Jack and I will wait in the shop." She headed for the door.

Jack didn't move. "I'd like to stay, if you don't mind."

"Yeah. I mind. Police business." Cocky upstart.

"Why don't we eat and then talk, Book?" Della asked, whisking a bowl of eggs.

Book reached over and turned off the flame beneath the omelet pan. "No, we'll talk now. And we'll talk alone."

He waited for Perry and Jack to leave the room before he looked to Della again. She stood in the corner where two of the aqua-tiled kitchen's countertops formed a right angle, and her expression told him he wouldn't like what she was going to say.

"You should have let Jack stay. He might have information you can use."

She was right. He didn't like it. "Does he?" he asked, his gut tightening.

"He might."

"But you don't know."

"Contrary to popular belief, Book, I don't know everything." She pushed away from the corner and crossed in front of him, making her way to the table.

She smelled like a field of flowers, something warm and purple and soft. He followed her, took the chair beside hers, staying close. "Tell me what you do know."

She related to him the same things she'd said on the phone earlier. This time, as he took notes, he pressed for specific details. On the ring, especially.

He'd get a sketch done and canvas area pawnshops to start. Nothing that took a lot of time away from his legitimate cases. Nothing that would get him written up for coloring outside the lines. Again.

"What is your department saying this time?"

"Not much." He didn't know why she asked when she already knew.

"Book, tell me the truth."

He closed his notebook, capped his pen and returned both to his coat's inside pocket. "We're not officially on this case. There hasn't been enough evidence to warrant our involvement."

"You're here on your own then?"

He was here because of her visions. But he was also here because of her. "It's no different than any other time."

She shook her head slowly. Tendrils of hair fell to curl around her face. She hooked her bare feet on the rung beneath his chair and leaned toward him, reaching out with one hand, pulling it back before he could wrap up her fingers with his.

"I never meant to be a burden to you. To cause you trouble at work, or with your peers." She laced her hands in her lap, looking up at him as if he were the only one with the answer to her prayers. "I hope you know that."

He shrugged, blowing it off because he didn't give a damn what anyone thought when it came to his dealings with Della. All that mattered was that she came to no harm. "It's no big deal. I'm more concerned with you staying safe."

Her laugh was as light as a breath of fresh air. "I'm not in any danger. I never have been."

"In the past, no. But this time your name is in the paper." He was going to skin alive one particular big-mouthed leaker—especially since the leak was nothing but gossip.

He'd never talked about the Eckhardt case or about

Della's newest visions. The leak made operations a laughingstock. "I'm sorry that happened. I can see the scum is already oozing out of the woodwork."

She laughed again and sat back. "You're talking about Jack, I presume. Though I'm quite sure he said he came from Texas, not out of the woodwork."

Book's mental gears whirred too loudly for him to process more than the facts. "He's from Texas?" Eckhardt was from Texas.

"I believe Perry said Austin. The man's family hired him. Apparently, they're quite unsatisfied with the progress being made through police channels."

Montgomery showing up here like he had gave further credence to what Della had seen. Yet it still wasn't enough for Book to open an official case. Unofficial, he could manage. "I suppose I should talk to him."

Again, Della leaned forward. "You had the chance, you know. Before you ran the poor man out of here."

"I don't like the thought of you becoming a victim. Of you being exploited." He didn't like the idea of a lot of things when it came to Della Brazille. The biggest one being the way he hadn't yet harnessed his balls and told her how important she was to him. "Finding Montgomery here on top of finding that headline this morning has not made for the best start to the day."

"I know what you need."

Oh, but she had no idea. It always left him stymied, how she could see violent crimes but never the soft spot in his heart.

Still, he shifted in his chair so that no personal space remained between them, so that when he breathed in, it was her scent filling his lungs.

"Yeah? What's that?" he asked, his heart beating so hard in his throat he couldn't even swallow.

"You need brunch." She patted his knee as if he were a child, then got up to finish cooking.

All he could do was sit there and battle the urge to walk out the door.

WHAT PERRY WANTED most of all was for Jack to go away. He disturbed her, and she did not like being disturbed. Especially when, after living a rather disturbing life, she was finally feeling the calm of things going her way.

She stood at the register in Sugar Blues, having just rung up a customer. It seemed a good place to stay, what with the long, glass-topped counter between her and Jack. Because now that the two of them were alone, her senses were ringing high and loud.

He closed the book on Reiki training through which he'd been leafing and made his way to the rear of the shop. Of course, she had to notice his walk, how he moved, all lanky and long and loose. She wasn't supposed to notice that about him, and she sure wasn't supposed to like it.

She sighed, obviously having listened too much to Sugar singing the blues, waxing eloquent about the handsome men who'd broken her heart. Jack stopped at the counter and picked up a tiny gold incense burner. Funny how he always had to have his hands on something, stroking, fondling.

Perry groaned, catching the forward progression of her thoughts one stroke too late. "If you break it, you've bought it."

"Yeah," he said, running his thumb over the Buddha's belly. "I saw the sign on the door. Do you really sell enough of this crap to stay in business?"

"Do you insult everyone you meet or is this special treatment only for me?"

"I just say what comes to me."

"Open mouth, insert foot?"

He shrugged. "Guess that's one way of looking at it."

She barely managed to keep herself from rolling her eyes. "But not your way."

"Sorry, no," he said, returning the burner to the counter and reaching for her blue-plumed pen.

She moved it out of his reach before he could grab it. "Do you think you could limit your touchy-feely habit to items you're going to buy?"

He laughed then, the sound deep and resonant like that of a bass guitar, one that vibrated through her, tickling, taunting, one she knew she was going to have a problem with if he stayed around for long.

Or not, she amended moments later, when he said, "There's nothing about this place that I buy. Horoscopes and healings and protection charms? What a bunch of—"

"A bunch of what?" She bristled further, not quite sure why she was letting him get to her when his opinion was one she'd run up against too many times to count. "A bunch of crap? A bunch of, what did you call it earlier, hocus-pocus?"

"You're going to tell me it's not? That you be-lieve—" he glanced at the cover of the book and read the copy "—I can learn how to create an electro-magnetic balance all the way to the cellular level in the physical body? Just by taking a couple of classes?"

She pruned her lips, then forced them to relax. "I believe there are many things not easily explained by conventional reasoning."

"Let me guess. You're a big *X-Files* fan."

This time she gave in, rolling her eyes. "Just my luck, stuck entertaining a smart-ass."

"Smart enough to know the difference between what's real and what isn't," he said, a brow going up and drawing her gaze to his lashes again.

"You think Detective Franklin would be here if Della's visions were fabricated? If he didn't have proof that what she sees is real?" Gah, but she hated finding intelligent minds closed.

"You tell me."

"What, and waste my breath? I think I'd rather show you," she said, having heard the faint croon of a female voice drifting down the stairs behind her.

He snorted. "I've been around the block, sister. I've pretty much seen it all."

"Ah, but have you listened to it?"

"Listened to what?"

Perry narrowed her gaze. "If I let you come around here, do you think you can keep your hands to yourself?"

The words left her mouth before she could stop them.

His eyes flashed, specks of silver bright in the deep dark gray. He let his gaze drop from her face to her shoulders before she glared and moved behind the cash register to hide.

He laughed again, shoved his hands into his jeans pockets and walked his lazy, loose and lanky way around to where she stood.

"Better?" he asked, once he was close enough to touch…if only she had the guts to reach out.

What would be better would be to start this day over and not have him show up to disturb her. "Yes. Now listen."

She backed toward the staircase and motioned him forward. Wariness in his expression, he did as she asked, stopping when she held up one hand.

"Listen," she whispered, standing on one side of the stairwell opening as he stood on the other. "Tell me what you hear."

He propped a shoulder against the wall and hung his head; she leaned into the corner, her hands stacked behind her.

The days just ain't the same…

The walls of the stairwell that rose to the second floor were brick, and on them hung framed photos of Sugar. At clubs in the old Storyville district, performing with Jelly Roll Morton and Johnny Dodds.

The sun hangs low and hangs dark…

More Sugar Babin memorabilia remained stored in the attic. LPs and costumes. Even her famous gold cigarette case and gnarled walking stick.

The nights never end, never fade…

Perry didn't know how Jack—how anyone—could deny the interaction between this world and those that lay beyond, when hearing Sugar sing.

Black is the color of my heart...

Nor did she understand why he wasn't saying anything. "Well?"

Still staring down at the floor, he shrugged. "Your aunt left a radio playing?"

"No." Perry shook her head. "That's Sugar."

"Another aunt?"

"This used to be where she lived. This building. She was a famous blues singer."

"So you pipe the music into the shop for old times' sake."

"No. That's Sugar singing." She waited and waited, but his expression never changed. "She died after a suspicious fall down the stairs. These stairs," she added, pointing.

"Then the piping's about exploiting the legend?"

It took all her control not to stomp her foot. "Jack, there is no piping. That singing you hear is Sugar's ghost."

3

WHAT A LOAD of hooey. "You're kidding me, right? A ghost?"

"Don't tell me you don't hear her."

"I hear music." He shrugged. That much was true. "It doesn't mean I buy into any ghost story."

Perry sighed and closed her eyes. "I should be used to this by now. I don't know why I let it get to me."

"Hey, it's got to be good for business." Jack backed up against the wall, keeping his hands in his pockets since she seemed bothered when he used them. "Adds to the woo-woo flavor of the place."

Perry pushed away from the corner and paced the length of the counter twice before she stopped to face him. "Believe or don't believe. It's no skin off my nose that you're lacking an open mind."

His mouth twisted to the right. "Guess I played hooky the day they passed out the gene."

"I wouldn't be surprised to find out you played hooky several days in a row."

That made him smile. "You think?"

"Yeah. I do." When she tossed back her hair, the strands of colored crystals dangling from her ears twinkled, speckling her cheeks with dots of blue and gold. "You missed good manners day, for one."

"Actually, that gene's only loose."

She gave him a measured glare. "There's a toolbox on the floor of the pantry."

"Thanks. I'll see what I can do about tightening it up before I head out."

"And when will that be?"

"I was hoping for brunch, at least." He wasn't really, considering he was still burning up inside from the gumbo. He just wasn't ready to leave. "And maybe more time with your aunt once the detective is through."

"I doubt she'll be able to tell you anything useful. Her visions aren't exactly newsreels."

"What are they?"

Perry boosted herself up onto the stool at the cash register. "It's hard to explain. Even to believers."

"The listening gene?" When she arched a brow, he went on. "I was there that day. It was handed out at the same time as the one for paying attention."

Her smile was slow to come but when it did, Jack felt as if he'd been poleaxed. It wasn't even about her mouth—though she did have a great one that sent his mind south—as much as it was about her eyes.

They were deep and dark, more black than brown, and they were sucking him down in a hurry. They were eyes he could drown in, dangerous and dazzling, which his experience told him meant deceptive as well.

"In that case, all I can tell you is that she sees flashes," she said, the smile fading. "Bits and pieces of clothing. Or a location. The last time she helped Book, she saw chickens."

O-kay. "Doesn't sound like a lot of help."

"Oh, but it was," she insisted, crossing one leg over the other. "The chickens she saw are only raised at two area farms. The police were able to close in quicker with that one bit of information added to what they already had."

Interesting. And legit enough that he could easily check it out. But he still wasn't buying the ghost. "Close in quicker on what?" When she hesitated, he prodded her with, "What was the case?"

She hopped down from the stool, turned to the counter and began to straighten the chains on a display of jeweled silver pendants. "It was infanticide, and it was ugly. If you want details, you're going to have to check newspaper archives."

"I'll do that."

"Fine. Just don't say a word about it to Della. She doesn't need to relive any of that."

The thought hadn't crossed his mind. "I won't. I promise. Pinky swear and everything."

Her hands stilled on the pendants, and it took a minute for her to respond. When she did, it was to turn slowly and face him, to wrap her arms around her middle, to take him in from head to toe—twice—and say, "I'm not so sure I want to make a pinky swear with you."

"Why not?" He pulled his hands from his pockets, hooked his thumbs in his belt loops, drawing her gaze.

Her throat worked as she swallowed. "With that

hands-on thing you have going, I'm not sure you can keep it to just a pinky."

She believed in ghosts and psychics and whatever the hell rune stones were, but the idea of holding his hand was too much for her? He took one step forward, offered her his little finger without saying a word.

He could tell by her hiss of breath that she was as bothered by his dare as by the thought of making physical contact, yet he was certain that what bothered her most of all was the quirk in her makeup that wouldn't let her walk away.

Thing was, it got to him, too—her hesitation, her unease—but in a way he'd bet cold hard cash was the polar opposite of hers. Even more so, however, he was caught off guard by her eyes and her mouth, and the fact that he couldn't remember the last time a woman had looked him over with such intensity.

She took a step toward him and lifted her hand, pinky extended. An inch and no more separated their fingers. At least an inch of actual, measurable space. What couldn't be measured was everything else keeping them apart. The unspoken words and the private thoughts and the truth of this step they were taking.

Then, before he could say anything or form another thought or even define what this particular truth was, she hooked him, her finger grabbing his and pulling tight. He grabbed harder, holding her there even when she gave a half-hearted tug for freedom.

"See?" She glared. "I knew you couldn't keep up your end of the bargain."

"Remind me again of the terms," he said, close

enough to see the spattering of freckles on her nose that she'd powdered away.

Close enough to smell the herbs in her shampoo, the coffee she'd had in the kitchen, her skin. "I've totally forgotten what—"

A loud crash came from the rear of the building— breaking glass, a thud—followed by Della's sharp cry, the detective's sharper curse and the *whack* of a door bouncing open on its hinges.

Perry nearly took off Jack's arm as she jerked her hand free from his and ran through the beaded curtain toward the kitchen.

He was right behind, and he heard her gasp when she stopped. He also came close to mowing her down. His hands on her shoulders steadied them both as they stared at the scene that had her shaking.

The back door stood wide open, the window shattered, shards of glass scattered across the floor. Detective Franklin was nowhere to be seen, while Della was in the process of boosting herself up onto the counter beside the sink to rinse blood from her foot.

"Oh, my God, Della." Perry rushed forward, broken glass crunching beneath her ankle boots. "What happened? Where's Book? Are you all right?"

"There. On the floor." Her hand shaking, Della pointed to the kitchen table. Jack saw what appeared to be a brick wrapped in newspaper. "Book said to leave it. He ran out to look for suspects."

"Why would anyone throw a brick through our window?" Perry's voice vibrated with anger and righteous concern. "Let me look at your foot."

Della turned on the water, sucking in a breath. "I jumped to dodge the brick, lost my balance and misstepped. I'll be fine. But I'm quite sure when Book unwraps it from the newspaper, we'll find this morning's headline inside."

"Someone is taking the story seriously," Jack said, feeling powerless when he was used to being in charge. "Where's your broom?"

"The closet next to the pantry," Perry said, waving him in that direction. "This is going to need stitches."

"Book said not to touch anything," Della insisted, though that didn't stop Jack.

"He can sweep up the glass," Book replied, coming back in through the door and snapping open his handkerchief. "I want to bag the brick and the paper in case we luck out and pick up any trace."

Trace? On something as innocuous as a broken window? Jack wondered how deeply the detective thought this case ran. Or if his attention was also personal.

"You think someone involved in the kidnapping is trying to keep Della out of the picture?" Perry asked, pulling a first aid kit from the drawer next to the sink.

"At the very least," Book said, dropping the brick into the paper bag Jack handed him from the pantry and turning to Della. "A patrol car's on the way. The officers will interview for witnesses. I want to get this bag to the lab, and the sooner I get it there—"

"Go, Book. Do what you need to do," Della said, grimacing as Perry wrapped her foot in gauze. "Perry can take me to the clinic to get this taken care of."

"Let me lock up the shop," Perry said, hurriedly heading that way. "Kachina is scheduled to come in today at two. We'll just close up until then."

"Kachina?" Jack asked.

"One of my employees," Della said, holding her injured foot in her lap as she waited for her niece to return.

Detective Franklin crossed the room, wrapped his arm around her and helped her down. "I'll have one of the officers stay here until you get back."

"No need," Jack said. This he could do. "I'll stay and get started on prepping to replace the glass."

"Jack, you don't have to—"

"I know I don't," he said, cutting Della off. "I want to."

"This way he'll have a legitimate excuse to snoop," Perry said, walking back into the kitchen, keys jangling in one hand. She stared at him, daring his denial.

He didn't give her one. All he said was, "The only thing I'll be snooping for is the toolbox. Which I remember you telling me was on the pantry floor."

"Listen, Jack. How about measuring to replace the whole door?" the detective asked after a telling pause. "The hinges and knob are shot. The wood is warped, and the whole thing is barely hanging on the frame."

"Not a problem." Jack swept the glass into a dustpan, dumping it into the trash. Perry was right, even while she was wrong. The repairs *would* give him a reason to hang around, which would give Della— hopefully—incentive to talk. "I'll pick up what I need when everyone's back."

"Jack, I can't ask you to do that," Della protested as both Book and Perry helped her to the door.

"You're not asking me to do anything." He stored the broom in the closet, pulled out the canister vacuum to give the floor a thorough once-over, raising his hand in an answering farewell to Book's nod of thanks.

Then he turned his attention to Perry, who had lingered behind. "I won't leave the kitchen while you're gone. I won't answer the phone. I won't snoop in cabinets. I won't touch a thing but the door."

He laughed to himself at the suspicious look with which she left him. But she truly had nothing to worry about. Getting the door replaced before nightfall would take all of his time. Besides, he'd much rather get the goods he needed directly from the women involved.

Especially the wild-haired gypsy.

HAVING SETTLED DELLA INTO her room's chintz-covered chaise lounge with a pot of tea, a romance novel and a pillow beneath her foot, Perry headed back to the kitchen to check on Jack's progress.

Three hours after leaving, she and her aunt had arrived home from the clinic—Della with eighteen stitches across the ball of her foot—to find him anxious to hit the hardware store. Giving him directions to the store she used, Della sent Jack on his way with her credit card, then called the manager to tell him to expect him.

Jack's having arrived in New Orleans driving an SUV meant Perry hadn't needed to find a truck to borrow, or wait to have the store deliver the new door—not to mention the fact that his being in the right place at the right time meant no exorbitant bill for emergency labor.

Jack Montgomery was turning out to be handy to have around, and she wasn't sure what to make of that.

Her father had been the only man she'd ever had in her life, and she'd lost him when she was ten. She'd come here to live with her aunt after her parents' death, and Della had ignored her childish whining and constant pleas to send her to public school.

Instead, her aunt had honored her parents' wishes, and Perry had spent the next eight years attending an all-girls private academy. After graduation, she'd taken a few courses at Loyola University, but never felt as if she and higher education made a good fit.

Hardly a revelation, considering the instruction she'd received from Della. Growing up under her tutelage was like sitting and learning at a master's feet—the main drawback being the social isolation and the lack of opportunities to mingle with men.

Stepping from the stairwell into the shop, Perry found herself puttering behind the counter instead of returning to the kitchen—a classic case of avoiding the man she'd left there. At least she was honest in not trying to fool herself that it was anything else.

She hated her obvious attraction to Jack because she wasn't sure what to do next. The men she had dated while attending university classes—boys, really, weren't they?—had given her a rather lopsided look at the opposite sex. Dating for them had been about how far they could get her to go.

With her aunt being a veritable French Quarter legend, Perry had earned the status of trophy lay once her name had become known. Even more humiliating had been finding out that because she wasn't laying anyone, she was ranked number one on the campus virgin watch.

And that was funny because she'd lost her virginity the summer before her freshman year to the only good man she'd ever known. Gary had not seen her as anyone but who she was. He'd loved her. He'd made love to her. He'd taught her about herself, things she could never have learned from her aunt because they were all about her enjoyment of sharing her life—and her body—with a man.

They'd spent a wonderful six months together—the best she'd even known. But then a job offer had taken Gary, who'd been eight years older, to Seattle. They were at different places in their lives, he'd told her. Devastated, she'd risen to the occasion with a surprising maturity, reminding him of her obligation to Della keeping her in New Orleans and wishing him all the best while her heart crumbled.

Allowing herself to dwell on what might have been with Gary, or later, on the bets being made behind her back, had been a waste of time. University had been the same, and so she'd moved on. For ten years now, she'd managed Sugar Blues, a full circle that brought her back to a life spent in the company of women— not such a bad thing, she supposed. Della didn't seem to have suffered for living her life alone.

Then again, she had definitely been filled with *joie*

de vivre since Detective Book Franklin had arrived on the scene. Strange, but Perry had always thought Della shied away from relationships because of her gift—not because she hadn't found a man to hold her interest.

And, of course, that brought Perry's mind back to Jack. She stopped futzing with the layout of the counter's incense cones and took a deep breath, forcing her feet to move. She walked into the kitchen to Jack bearing the brunt of the door's weight on one shoulder.

"Hey, there you are," he said. "Could you hand me that hammer?"

"Sure," she answered without thinking, adding, "The claw or the ball pin?"

"Either one'll work," he said, taking it from her hand with a wink. "Gotta love a woman who knows her way around tools."

She ignored the double entendre. "This is a do-it-yourself sort of household."

"You live here, too, then?"

She shook her head, leaned against the counter nearest the doorway, shivering a bit from the breeze. "I used to. Not anymore. I have a townhouse near Jackson Square."

"Hmm. I was down there earlier." *Whack! Whack!* "Ate lunch at a place called Café Eros. Actually, that's where I picked up the newspaper."

Did she dare tell him? It wasn't like she was unlisted or anything. "Actually, that's where I live. The Court du Chaud. The café sits at the entrance."

"Small world, huh?"

Too small, she wanted to say. But she didn't say

anything because as he lifted the old door free, she was caught by the ripple of muscles across his back.

He'd pulled off his hoodie since his return from the store and was now working in his T-shirt and jeans. The heavier garment had covered his upper physique; the white cotton T-shirt covered it in a way that was all about showing it off.

When he reached up, the shirt went with him, baring a strip of skin above his belt. Not more than an inch, maybe only a half, there at the small of his back. It was enough. She forgot to breathe for so long that her lungs burned when she finally filled them.

She was so out of her league.

"I can always leave," she said, hoping he'd agree. *Please let him agree*. If she stayed even a few minutes longer, it was going to be too long. It was going to be too late. "If you have the place to yourself, you can work without being distracted."

"I'd rather you stay." *Whack! Whack!* "I like the way you distract me."

No, no, no. After that infamous pinky swear, flirting from this man was one thing she did not need. "If I distract you, it will take you longer to get finished. If I leave you alone, you'll be done and out of here in no time."

He turned then, resting the door against the frame. His T-shirt had hiked up in the front as well. The strip of skin bared there was just as sleek and tight as the other, only this one was marked down the center by a line of dark hair.

"Is this about protecting your aunt? Or is there

another reason you want me out of here?" He stepped away from the door, crouched at the toolbox left open on the floor. "It's obvious you think I'm here to hurt her. Or use her. Which I'm not."

Perry hopped up to sit on the counter. "You came in guns blazing. Whether or not you meant to hurt her isn't the point."

Jack's mouth twisted. "Bad first impression, huh?"

"Oh, yeah." She nodded. "So bad."

"Well," he said, picking up a paint scraper, discarding an awl. "I'm doing my best here to make amends."

She remained silent, and that caused him to look up from where he'd been searching through the tools.

His eyes glittered. The shadow of his beard appeared darker from this angle. Dark and sexy, giving him an edgy sense of heat. It was a look that was predatory—not one she'd expect in a handyman.

Then again, that's not what he was, was it?

"Della is the only family I have. Protecting her is what I do." And it wasn't a need to protect based on some misplaced sense of failing to keep her parents safe.

Perry didn't know what she'd do if she lost Della.

Jack got to his feet. "There's nothing wrong with being protective. I may be skeptical about ghosts and psychics—"

"Skeptical or disbelieving?"

His expression spoke before he did. "Same thing, isn't it?"

"And you don't think that hurts her?" This is what no one seemed to get. Della didn't spend her time casually tossing around her visions like discount coupons for anyone interested in what she was selling.

Her visions were who she was. Rejecting her gift equaled rejecting her.

And Perry knew exactly the hurt that caused her aunt, no matter Della's stiff upper lip.

Jack turned back to the door, knocking loose chips and clumps of decades-old paint. "I'm not a physical threat. Whether or not I buy into what she says she sees—"

"Jack! This isn't about what she says. It's about what she sees. Do you not get that? It's real. The police have been able to use her visions. That's also real."

He threw the scraper at the toolbox; it clattered across the kitchen floor, but she doubted he even noticed. He was busy with the old door, picking it up and hefting it outside where she heard it splinter across the courtyard.

She started to jump down from the counter, was stopped when he swung out of the doorway toward her and blocked her with his hands on the counter at her hips.

His chest heaved. His pulse throbbed at his temples. The tendons in his neck stood in sharp relief, and she swore his nostrils flared.

She didn't know this man at all, yet she didn't feel the least bit afraid. Only curious as to what her words had set off inside him.

"Listen to me, Perry. There is only one thing here that's real," he said, his tone harsh, his words measured. He held her gaze for several long seconds. She didn't flinch, and he held it still.

But then the tic in his jaw lessened, and the sense of imminent explosion faded away. He dropped his gaze from hers to the charm she wore around her neck. And when he spoke again he did so with a bit of a tremor in his voice.

"The only thing real right now is that I've got a door to fix and not much daylight left to do it. So, yeah. You're right. It's probably best if I finish up without you around to distract me."

4

JACK ENDED UP spending the night in his sleeping bag
on Della Brazille's kitchen floor. Perry had left him
alone to finish the door as he'd requested, never breathing another word.

She'd stayed in the shop until closing time—he'd
heard her chatting with customers and with the woman
he supposed was Kachina—returning to the kitchen
around seven to make soup and sandwiches for herself
and her aunt.

She'd carried the meal upstairs on a tray, leaving
him a sandwich in the refrigerator next to a bowl of
soup.

He hadn't even known they were there, had only
found them when he'd decided to scrounge for a bite,
and took the offering as a sign that she'd forgiven him
for blowing up at her earlier in the day. He certainly
hadn't meant to, and had only exhaustion and frustration to blame.

He owed Perry an apology. He'd deliver it
tomorrow, having stayed the night because he couldn't
get the door lock to hold. He'd fought the deadbolt
until after midnight, but needed tools neither he nor the

Brazille women had on hand. Detective Franklin had been right about the state of the door, but the building's brick walls weren't so shabby.

Besides, the new door needed a coat of paint, and he'd have to check with the owners on that tomorrow. If he ever saw either one of them again. If they even let him stick around to finish the job. If they didn't decide he was only staying to snoop, and kick him to the curb.

He shouldn't have gone off on Perry the way he had. Didn't it just figure that the anger he tried to keep buried would come back to life in a haunted house owned by a psychic? One who used her supposed visions to help the police—and whose niece Jack wouldn't mind sharing his sleeping bag with.

He couldn't help it. Ever since that ridiculous pinky swear, all he could think about was her eyes. Okay. Not so much just her eyes. Her mouth was an equally big part of his lust. He wanted to kiss her, but not half as much as he wanted to feel her mouth on his body.

She'd noticed his hands-on habit, commented on it more than once. What she didn't know—couldn't know—was how much he ached to have a woman's hands on him. It had been a long time since he'd spent enough time in bed with a woman to give her the chance to touch him. Usually he was in and out and on his way before he had a chance to think.

He wanted to feel Perry's hands, her long, strong fingers, her palms, the nails she kept short. But lying here on his back, his head pillowed on his stacked wrists, staring up at the kitchen ceiling with sweat slick on his skin, was not the time or place to be working himself up. Especially since what he wanted from her went beyond the physical.

Her loyalty to her aunt said a lot about the woman Perry was. He had yet to learn much more, but he liked that particular detail—even if it was a big part of why, as long as he was here, he knew they'd continue to butt heads.

So far, Perry had seemed unwilling to consider that he might have a reason to doubt what she held to be the truth. And since he wasn't exactly in touch with his feminine side and prone to blurt out his feelings, well, they'd have to figure out how best to come to a meeting of the minds.

Because it had to happen. What he wanted to know was how Della Brazille was connected to Dayton Eckhardt. And he wasn't leaving until he got the answers he'd come to New Orleans to get.

He had just closed his eyes and was drifting off when he heard the beaded curtain between the shop and the kitchen jangle as someone walked through. Since no one knew he'd made himself at home in the kitchen, he sat up.

And as soon as he saw the dark cloud of Perry's hair turned to a bright blue-black by the light from the sink's window, he made himself known. "Perry, don't freak. I'm camped out by the door."

The tray of dishes she was carrying didn't even rattle when she set it on the counter. "I thought you might be. Your SUV's still outside."

Why was he not surprised? "You've been watching for me to leave?"

"Not for you to leave. Just watching." She set the plates and bowls in the sink, rinsed and dried the tray.

He thought about getting to his feet, helping out, seeing if he could steer the conversation where he wanted it by showing her that he was as handy when it came to doing dishes as he was with replacing doors.

But then he thought better.

She'd been watching to see if he'd left. She knew that he hadn't, and yet here she was. Not scared, not running away. He hadn't forgotten about that pinky swear made behind the counter in Sugar Blues, and was pretty damn sure that was a big part of Perry being here now.

Here in the dark, in the middle of the night, with no one else around to talk her out of anything. And so he stayed where he was and waited to see what she had on her mind. In another minute, she surprised the hell out of him by joining him on the floor.

Resting against a wall of cabinets, she pulled her knees to her chest, wrapped her arms around them. She was wearing a full skirt again, this one printed with the reds, yellows, oranges and browns of autumn. Gold threads outlining the leaves sparkled where they were spun.

She cleared her throat, breathed deeply. "I don't know why I'm telling you this except that it's what I had wanted to tell you before."

When she paused, he shifted to sit straighter. "I'm listening."

"I almost think it's easier to talk to you in the dark," she said, laughing so softly he strained to hear.

He tried to set her at ease. "I've been told I'm hard on the eyes."

"Then you've been lied to," she replied without hesitation. "You are very…disturbing. You make me forget what I'm trying to say."

He filed away the ammunition to use later, waited for her to go on.

"Here's the thing, Jack," she said, when she finally did. "I've lived with Della since I was ten years old. I've seen how she suffers because of this gift."

"Physically?"

She nodded. Her face remained in shadow; he saw the movement in the light through her hair. "Killer migraines that exhaust her for days. And then there's the worry over the meaning of what she sees. Whether or not a life might be lost if no one can make sense of her visions."

"Does that actually happen?"

"We have no way of knowing."

Made sense, he supposed. "If there's nothing she can do or control, then it seems like a waste to worry."

"A waste of what?"

He shrugged, uncertain how far beneath the surface the ice in her voice ran. "Her energy? Her time?"

"Della's not like that. She's not so…cruel."

"It's practical, not cruel."

Again with the shake of the head. "I knew you wouldn't get it."

He wasn't being hardheaded on purpose. It was just that he didn't put stock in what he couldn't see, what he couldn't touch. "Try me. Start from the beginning.

You said you went to live with Della when you were ten."

"Yes. After my parents' death."

Wow. Not good. "That must've been tough, losing them both, being so young."

She tugged her skirt tighter over her knees. "It was. I was pretty confused for a while. But Della had always been a big part of my life, almost more like my older sister than my father's younger one."

"Anyone else in the family…special?"

"You mean psychic?" she asked, when he bobbled the word. "Your true colors are showing, Jack."

"I wasn't trying to hide them." Honest enough. He was who he was and knew quite well where he'd come from, what experiences had made him, which ones he would always regret. "'Course I doubt they're as bright as that skirt you're wearing."

"Don't try to change the subject."

Was that what he was doing? "I was just saying—"

"You were not saying. You were totally avoiding having the word psychic come out of your mouth."

"I believe in what I can see, what I can hear and taste and smell and get my hands on."

She gave a snort. "Especially that hands part."

He wasn't going to deny it. "You grew up exposed to your aunt's visions. I wouldn't expect you to do anything but defend her."

She cocked her head to one side, let go of her knees and straightened out her legs beside his. "And what were you exposed to growing up? What happened to close your mind so completely?"

Life, he wanted to say. Deception and lies and bone-deep betrayal. Instead, he tossed back the top of the sleeping bag. He wanted to see if she would move away without the barrier between her legs and his.

But she stayed where she was, waiting, and he ended up giving her some of what she wanted to know, leaving out what he knew about cruelty. "I was exposed to baseball, hot dogs, apple pie, and the United States Marine Corps. And my mind, as far as I can tell, is wide open. Not sure I'd still be here, otherwise."

Her bracelets jingled softly as she toyed with the fabric of her skirt. "I thought you were here because of the door."

"I thought you were here to do dishes."

"They'll still be there in the morning."

"So will the door." And since they were on an honesty roll… "What's the relationship between your aunt and Dayton Eckhardt?"

That brought her head up. "Why do you think there is one?"

"She's seeing him." He shrugged. "Or at least things related to him."

Perry's snort told him what she thought of that. "She saw things related to last summer's killings. That didn't mean she had a relationship with the psycho."

Jack still wasn't buying it. "The headline was designed to put her in the limelight. Why?"

"Unwanted limelight, and how should I know?" She raised her voice. "I had nothing to do with it."

He pushed harder. "The brick, then. Why would anyone feel the need to warn her off?"

"Maybe because they don't like her being in the limelight, either."

More like they didn't want the kidnapping in the limelight, and the headline gave them the connection to Della. That connection was the key. The big fat who, where, when, how and why. "We're dealing with two separate elements here."

"How so?"

"The brick is an obvious warning. What I want to know is, why the headline? Who would benefit from Della's exposure?"

"A reporter looking for a scoop?"

"But there's been no hard evidence of Eckhardt crossing into Louisiana. The authorities in Texas are still operating under the assumption that they'll find him on their side of the state line. Unless…"

"Unless what?" she prodded.

"Unless the reporter knows better." Jack grabbed for his duffel bag, pulled out a flashlight and the newspaper.

He scanned the story that was nothing but the facts of the case gleaned from the ongoing investigation in Texas, coupled with a larger profile of Eckton Computing's roots in New Orleans, and the industry buzz about a new software system that would blow competitors away.

"Do you want me to turn on the light?" Perry asked.

He shook his head. "No, this is fine. This reporter, Dawn Taylor. The name ring a bell?"

"Not at all, but I'll ask Della in the morning."

Morning. Crap. It was the middle of the night. He'd

been about to head to the *Times-Picayune* offices. He stored the paper, waited to switch off the flashlight. "I'll go talk to Ms. Taylor before I pick up your paint."

"Paint?"

"For the door. I'm assuming you'll want blue?"

She gave him another soft laugh in response. "I'll have to ask Della about that, too. I don't live here anymore, remember?"

But she had lived here once with the woman who'd raised her. No wonder she seemed perfectly at home. "Do you stay here often?"

"Not really, though I still have a room upstairs. Lately I've been here a lot, but that's because of Della not feeling well."

"Guess that puts a strain on the business."

She laughed at that. "Only because we have to scramble to reschedule her appointments. Trust me. Della's clients are that loyal. They'll wait. In the meantime, the shop does a great business, and Kachina has her own fanatical following."

She paused, and when he didn't respond, she went on, chuckling beneath her breath. "Welcome to N'Awlins, Jack Montgomery. You're sleeping on the kitchen floor of a woman who's a local legend."

A state of things he would never understand.

"Though you know," Perry continued, scrambling to her feet, her bracelets tinkling, her skirt sweeping over him and the floor. "There is a single bed you could use. It's around the corner and down the hall from the bathroom. In the utility room." She held out her hand. "C'mon. I'll show you."

He took her hand, not needing the help, just wanting to touch her, and stood. "It's better that I stay here. The door lacking a lock and all."

She waved off the offer. "Book has a patrol car making extra rounds, you know."

"And you know it wouldn't take a lot of brains to watch and time a break-in," he said, still holding on to her hand.

She seemed to realize it at the same time, and her fingers stiffened. She pulled free, though with a hint of reluctance, and walked through the dark room to the sink where she washed the dishes she'd left there.

Jack watched her, the unhurried movements of her hands in the running water, the light from the moon spilling through the sink's window and giving him a better look at the tank top she wore.

The neckline didn't scoop particularly low, but it didn't need to. The fabric fit to show the fullness of her breasts, the curve of her waist, the strength in her shoulders and her spine.

He moved closer, leaning an elbow on the countertop and watching her, the way her hands slowed when she realized he was there, the way she tried not to smile but ended up giving in as she put the last bowl in the drainer.

"If you wanted to shower or anything while I'm down here, feel free." She glanced over. "I can wedge a chair beneath the doorknob. Keep out the bad guys."

"And if someone manages to shove through your wimpy security measures?"

She turned off the water, dried her hands. "The toolbox is still handy. I'll keep a hammer close by."

"Hmm." She was trying too hard to get rid of him. "I smell that bad, do I?"

"No, you just look a little fuzzy," she said, pressing her palm to his cheek. "Cleaning up might help you sleep better. It always works wonders for me."

He stopped breathing, waiting, certain that any moment she'd drop her hand. She'd back away. She'd give him a hard shove toward the door and out of her life. But she didn't do any of the above.

Instead, she stepped closer, stroked her fingers close to his ear and said, "Listen."

He couldn't hear a thing but his own labored breathing and the rolling-thunder beat of his heart. "I don't hear anything."

"Are you sure?" This time she whispered, ran her fingertips over the shell of his ear. "Be very quiet. Close your eyes."

He did both. He stood still. He was aware of nothing but Perry in the kitchen.

Her fingers were cool, her wrist warm where it grazed his cheek. Her hand smelled like lemony dish soap, but he caught a hint of her spicy scent beneath.

"Do you hear her now, Jack? Do you hear her singing? Pining for the lover who done her wrong?"

Ah. *Her.* The ghost. He opened his eyes, saw nothing but Perry, heard only her whisper's echo. "I hear an occasional car on the street outside. I hear your bracelets. I hear both of us having trouble breathing."

Her hand drifted down his neck to his shoulder. "I think you're imagining things."

"And you're not?"

She shook her head, squeezed his biceps, his forearm, finally his fingers as she laced them through hers. "C'mon. I'll prove it to you."

He didn't put up any fight at all as she tugged him out of the kitchen and through the beaded curtain. The streetlight from the corner shone through the store's front windows, glittering off the jewels and crystals scattered around the room.

It was an eerie sight, a magical and otherworldly sensation, surrounded as they were by darkness while vibrant colors flashed and sparked with no reason or rhyme.

Perry had stopped when he'd stopped. She stood now, watching him take in the fairy tale of colors and shapes, squeezing his hand when he shook his head.

"See what happens when you open your mind, Jack? Isn't it beautiful?"

Her voice was beautiful, and he couldn't help but turn toward her when she spoke. The room's kaleidoscope of colors swirled in her eyes, but that didn't stop him from bursting her bubble. "It's refracted light, Perry. Not bluebirds flying over a rainbow."

She smacked his shoulder teasingly with her free hand, leaned in close and whispered, "Don't you get tired of digging through the barrel for the bad apple?"

He brought her flush to his body. "What I get tired of is people not buying into the truth because they don't like what they see."

And the truth right now was that the threat to Della wasn't the threat on either of their minds.

He saw the mirror of his thoughts in Perry's eyes, the absolute honesty of this uneasy attraction weighing heavy between them.

Her throat worked as she swallowed. Her eyes, already large and dark, drank him in. She wet her lips, drawing his gaze to her mouth.

"Jack?"

"Perry?"

"Do you hear it now?"

"Hear what?"

"The truth."

"Is that what you call it?" he asked, hearing nothing but the rush of blood to his head.

She leaned in, brushed her lips to his. "I can hear it. Doesn't that mean that it's true?"

He slid their joined hands to the small of her back and pressed her body closer. She was soft and pliable, molding herself to him, fitting him like his favorite pair of worn jeans.

"Yeah, sure." He breathed the words against her mouth, not even certain what it was either one of them was saying. He was too full of feeling to think. "It's the truth."

She tightened her fingers laced with his, placed her other hand on his chest where his heart was working on a chain gang. "Well, good. There may be hope for you after all, now that you've come around to my way of thinking."

He had? When had that happened? he wondered, threading his fingers into her hair. "How so?"

Her hand rose higher, her fingertips pressing into

the tendons of his neck, her lips nipping at the corner of his. "I can tell you. Or you can kiss me."

As if that was even a choice.

He canted his head to the side where she waited and covered her mouth with his. It was a soft kiss, lips teasing and rubbing. A light nuzzling pressure. Her optimism working to loosen his pessimism while all he cared about was her taste.

She tasted good. She tasted sweet. When he nudged her lips with his tongue, she opened to let him have her. And then she kissed him back, pulling her hand from his and lacing her fingers at his nape.

She held him there tightly, sliding her tongue into his mouth to curl around his, massaging his neck with her thumbs, moving into his body…

No one would know if she kissed him.

No one would need find out. If she slipped up behind him while he sat there tuning his sax and planted her lips on his neck. Just to let him know she was around. Just to make sure he understood how often he played in her mind.

She'd been waiting, wanting a quiet moment, a private moment. The sort that came only when the club had closed down for the night, when the crowd had come and long gone. When everyone else in the band had packed it in, and Blind Billy had nothing more on his mind than wiping down the bar and counting up the night's take.

Her skirt swished against the velvet curtain as she stepped back onto the stage. The lights were out. Drake didn't need them for what he was doing, making sure his instrument was in fine working order, a necessity after the way he'd treated his baby tonight. She could still feel that mournful wail raising goose bumps all over her skin.

His head was down when she reached him, bent forward as he fondled the instrument. She could smell him. The smoke and the sweat, the bite of gin. The shiver that hit her took a whole lot of effort to suppress. She leaned down, blew against the shell of his ear, let her lips linger there at the base of his skull for no more than the length of a breath.

He straightened slowly and turned, and then gave her the smoky smile she'd wanted to feel forever. And she swore her heart forgot how to beat when he said, "Sweet Sugar Babin. Kissin' on me like that. What in the world would your husband say?"

5

JACK GROWLED, and it wasn't a very nice sound. It was the sound of his impatience, his frustration, his inability to be polite and still tell her to take off her clothes.

The kiss that had started out as a simple connection no longer was. It was about complications and how far they were going to go.

He made his first effort at finding out by bunching the material of her skirt into his fist at her hip. But she was wearing a hell of a lot of fabric and his hand was only so big. He wasn't getting anywhere and hated to stop.

Perry put him out of his misery with a sound that was half chuckle and half sigh before wiggling against him until he dropped her skirt. When he started to remind her that he had come around to her way of thinking after all, she pressed a finger to his lips and shushed him.

"This is the best part."

Or so he'd been on his way to find out before her skirt got in the way. She turned around then, tucked her head underneath his chin and snuggled her back to his front. And because it seemed like what he was meant to do, he wrapped his arms around her waist and held her.

It was seconds later when he was settling in to test the waters, when his focus along with his blood had begun the slow return trip to his head, when he realized exactly how perfectly her body fit his that he heard it. The singing. The low smoky voice lamenting love gone wrong.

That was her reason for bringing him here. It wasn't about showing him the shop at night or wanting to jump his bones. A trick, that's what it was. Another lame attempt to convince him the stairwell was haunted. To get him to…come around to her way of thinking.

Hell on freakin' wheels. A part of him raged at the deception. She could have brought him out here and told him to listen without the hot and heavy act. Thing was, he would swear on the closest voodoo priest that she hadn't been acting.

But then all his pondering over the ins and outs came to a screeching halt. Because he wasn't just hearing the ghost. He was seeing her.

He and Perry stood behind the counter, five feet from the corner where the frame around the stairwell's entrance no longer held a door. The outside wall between the first floor and the landing shared the exterior's brick.

And that was where Jack saw the light.

Not a direct source like a lamp or a flashlight or even a flickering candle flame. This was a wisp. And it floated. Floated and swirled over what he swore was a woman's figure in a long, formfitting dress.

He stepped from behind Perry, but she grabbed his

elbow and stopped him from moving closer. He frowned, but he didn't argue. He was too busy arguing with himself.

He could not believe, did not believe, that he was seeing what he was seeing. It had to be the same trick of the light from earlier, the one that had turned the shop into Munchkin Land. He wasn't buying that he was seeing a ghost. No flippin' way.

"I've only seen her three or four times in my life," Perry whispered. "Della's seen her more, but then she's lived here longer than I did. This was the apartment building where she and my father grew up long before she opened Sugar Blues."

He filed that away, still certain this was all about boxes with false bottoms and suspended panels he couldn't see. "She died here, you said. The singer?"

Still holding on to his arm, Perry nodded. "From a fall down the stairs. Though everything pointed to the fall being suspicious."

"Was there an investigation?" he asked, watching the ebb and flow of the ethereal light, listening to the faint murmur of song.

"A cursory one is all I found records of."

"You've researched the death?"

Again, she nodded. "You live with a ghost, you get curious."

In the next second, the song ceased as abruptly as if someone had turned off a CD player. The stairwell went dark in a flash. It was the strangest thing Jack had seen in a while—at least the strangest he wasn't able to explain.

Except the explanation became clear in the next moment when the sudden loud thump that followed turned out to be Della hobbling down the stairs.

Perry rushed forward. "You're supposed to be asleep."

"I was. I think it was Sugar who woke me," Della said, leaning heavily against Perry until Jack moved forward to take her weight. "Jack. You're still here."

"He was camping out in the kitchen in lieu of a lock on the door," Perry said, brushing loose hair back from her aunt's forehead.

"I'll finish with the deadbolt tomorrow," he said, his arm around Della's waist. "And pick up paint once you tell me what color."

"Oh, Jack," Della said, her brow lined with worry. "I'm afraid I have bad news. I believe Dayton Eckhardt may be dead."

IT WAS FOUR in the morning when Perry helped Jack get Della settled in the kitchen. She sat in one chair, propped her bandaged foot in another. Once she was situated, Jack rolled up his sleeping bag and carried it out to his SUV. Perry put on a pot of coffee.

She doubted any of them had plans to go back to sleep, then wondered if Jack had slept at all. He'd been wide awake when she'd come downstairs an hour ago, and he'd certainly shown no signs of being tired since.

She could *not* believe that she'd kissed him, or the way she'd tried so desperately to crawl into his clothes and down his throat. She'd met him at most eighteen hours ago, yet had gone after him like she hadn't had a man in, well, longer than she cared to admit.

It wasn't like Sugar Blues was a convent; she waited on plenty of male customers, flirted with more than a few. Then there were her male neighbors at Court du Chaud, with whom she teased and bantered regularly. And, of course, the male friends she'd made while living and working in the French Quarter.

But it had been many years since there'd been a man who lit the spark necessary for her to want to take things further.

Jack did. And in a very big way.

Standing in front of the steaming coffeemaker as the carafe filled, she cursed her renegade thoughts. She didn't like having to force her mind away from kissing Jack to focus on her aunt's needs.

Neither did she like the way Della's revelation had put a huge scowl on Jack's face before he packed up his gear. The truth was she didn't like thinking about Jack at all. Except that was a big fat lie.

Pulling three mugs down from the cupboard, Perry glanced to the side and caught her aunt's gaze. "How's your foot?"

"It hurts, but I'll be fine," Della said, brushing away the concept of pain as nothing.

Perry looked up at the clock on the wall behind the table. "You're due for another pain pill."

"And I took it before I came downstairs." Della repositioned the cushion beneath her heel. "What I want to know is what I interrupted by doing so?"

Perry felt her color rise. "Nothing, what do you mean?"

"You know exactly what I mean." Della arched a

wise brow. "What's going on with you and our new handyman?"

"He's not new, he's temporary, and I was trying to get him to open his mind about Sugar."

"A worthless endeavor, of which you should be well aware," Della said with a sigh. "Perry, sweetie, you can't force anyone to see what they don't want to see."

"I know." And she did. It was just hard to believe Jack—or anyone—couldn't see the same things that were so clear and so real to her. She poured her aunt's coffee. "He may not have opened his mind completely, but he knew she was there."

"He told you that?" Della asked, taking the cup from Perry's hand.

"No. But I could tell. She wasn't just singing this time. We saw her." Perry picked up her own cup at the same time Jack walked back through the door.

"I'm not surprised that you did," Della said.

Perry's only response was to offer coffee to Jack. He took the mug, asked, "Did what?" then blew across the surface and sipped.

"Saw Sugar," Perry replied, watching his expression as she brought her own mug to her mouth.

He didn't respond except to move to the table and pull out a chair opposite Della's. Once he sat, he still didn't say a word about having seen Sugar's ghost.

In fact, he seemed to dismiss both the subject and the incident without another thought, turning to Della to ask, "What makes you think Eckhardt is dead?"

Della cradled her mug and frowned as she stared down. "The intensity of the visions. Perry can tell you that when they're at their worst, I can be out of commission for hours."

When Jack looked over, Perry nodded, causing him to narrow his mouth and prompt Della further. "So what's different now?"

"I hate to say it, but it's been the case that the less painful the visions, the larger the threat or the more—" she fluttered one hand, then used it to push strands of hair from her face "—the more violent the outcome."

Jack brought his mug to his mouth, held it there but didn't drink. "I'd think the opposite would be true."

"That would seem to be the way of things if this gift had any basis in logic. But it's nothing I can control or anticipate."

"The sign on the front of the shop. You do readings, right?"

"Yes, but that's a more focused application of my gift. What comes to me in visions is nothing over which I have any discipline."

"Does the name Dawn Taylor mean anything to you?" he asked, with a quick change of subject.

She frowned as she thought, then shook her head. "I don't think so. Should it?"

"She's the reporter who wrote the story connecting you to Eckhardt," Perry said, joining them at the table. "Jack plans to ask her a few questions today."

"I wish I could give you something concrete to work with, Jack. Or that I had better news," Della said, wincing as she shifted her foot.

But Jack was intent on his coffee and seemed a

thousand miles away. "Perry said I could use the bathroom down here to clean up."

"Oh, of course," Della said, returning her cup to the table. "Please, make yourself at home. Especially after all the help you've been."

Jack snorted. "I haven't been that much. The door still needs to be painted and the deadbolt installed."

"Which will take too much time out of your day when you have an investigation to conduct. You do that, go about your business. I'll call my regular repair service."

"No," he argued. "I'll pick up the paint while I'm out and finish with the door this afternoon."

Perry silently wondered about his insistence. If he was that interested in seeing to the repairs, or if there was something else he wanted from Della. If there was more to his visit than he'd yet to reveal…unless he was actually considering their kiss in his decision to hang around.

She couldn't gauge anything by his expression, but kept her gaze on his face when she said, "I offered him the bed in the utility room."

"Where are you staying while you're in town, Jack?"

"Nowhere yet. I just got here this morning. Uh, yesterday morning."

"Well, the utility room's not much, but you're welcome to it. If Perry wasn't using her old bedroom upstairs, I'd offer you that."

"Don't worry about me. I'll find a place—"

"You could stay at mine," Perry put in before

thinking about what she was saying. Having Jack out of temptation's reach felt so much safer than having him here.

"That would be the perfect solution. You could keep an eye on Perry's place while she keeps an eye on me." Fighting a sly smile, Della reached over, patted then squeezed his forearm.

But before either Perry or Jack could reply, the sly smile disappeared. Della's hand began to shake. And the look that came over her face couldn't be described as anything but abject horror.

"Oh, Jack. I'm sorry. So very sorry. No man should ever suffer so."

JACK'S VISIT WITH Dawn Taylor had been a bust. The woman had fit him in between two phone calls while standing behind her journalistic integrity and insistence on protecting her sources.

He'd left after fifteen minutes of working for nothing, figuring he'd do better online starting with the *Times-Picayune* archives. All he needed was a Wi-Fi connection for his laptop. Then again, he could deal with dial-up if that was all he'd have at Perry's.

Parking his SUV in the space behind her townhouse, he tried not to think about what Della Brazille had seen in her kitchen when squeezing his arm. Or what she thought she'd seen, because he had a hard time believing she'd seen anything at all. Especially not the truth.

He didn't talk to anyone about his tour of duty. About being recruited into special ops and assigned to a detachment based on psyche tests and stamina and weapons proficiency, when in reality he'd been twenty-two years old and still struggling with the rift in his family caused by his decision to join the Corps.

There was nothing about him exceptional enough to have caught anyone's eye. He should've been able to serve his four years and go home, but he'd stayed for twelve. He'd seen things he didn't want to talk about, done things he didn't want anyone to know. Lived through things no one ever should.

Yet with no more than the touch of her hand to his arm, Della Brazille had divined everything…unless what she'd seen had been the prelude to his long military stint. The choice his father had given him that hadn't been a choice, but an ultimatum he'd lacked the maturity to face.

His sister's battle with Batten disease, a fatal, inherited disorder of the nervous system, had taken her and his mother to Johns Hopkins and Baltimore during his senior year. His father had kept an apartment in Austin, though he'd spent only a night or two there each week. That left Jack, at seventeen, virtually on his own.

The agreement was that he'd rejoin the family after graduation and attend college in the northeast. It didn't matter that he'd been accepted at UT, or that he'd counted on being a longhorn since the first time he'd seen Bevo, the school's mascot, as a kid. The family needed to be together, his father said. All of them. For his sister's sake.

When the time had come for him to move, Jack had balked. His group of friends in Austin—the deck—had been the only family he'd known for the twelve months prior. They'd been the family he'd counted on while his parents devoted one-hundred-and-ten percent of their time to his sister.

They had, in fact, shown him the truth of what family was all about. He'd fit in. He'd played a part. He'd eaten Thanksgiving dinner with the Schneiders, Randy's family. He'd gone skiing over Christmas vacation with Ben and the rest of the Tannens. All of them—Jack, Ben, Randy, Quentin and Heidi—had spent spring break at South Padre Island. And they'd kept each other out of trouble and on the straight and narrow throughout their senior year.

He hadn't been the one whose opinions were never sought, whose questions were never considered, whose needs had taken a back seat. Who'd been as invisible as Sugar Blues' ghost. Janie had been sick for a very long time. Jack had ceased to exist in his parents' eyes, way before the final move.

Staying in Texas wasn't a show of rebellion. It was a show of standing on his own, of being the adult he'd been told for years he needed to be. His father had refused to allow it. He would move from Austin or there would be no money for school. Jack had been left little choice, his longhorn dream punted to the far side of a four-year enlistment.

Four years, that became eight that became twelve. Janie had died during the fifth year. She'd been only sixteen to his twenty-two. He hadn't seen his parents since attending her funeral and standing alone at the rear of the church. Even now, thinking of her life cut so short, of her suffering…he choked, swallowed, shook off the emotion. He could never take back that he hadn't been there for her. And sharing his regrets wouldn't do anyone any good.

If that was what Della had seen…well, whatever it was, he hoped she'd keep her secrets to herself and not share them with Perry.

Pity was the last thing he wanted.

He hadn't seen either woman when he'd dropped back by Sugar Blues to finish up with the door. It had taken him the better part of the afternoon to install the dead bolt and put up a coat of primer. He could've done more, but rain was threatening, and he was beyond beat.

Kachina Leaping Water, the Native American seer Della employed, had been the one to give him the key to Perry's townhouse when he'd gone into the shop to find her. He hadn't needed directions; he remembered both Court du Chaud and Café Eros. He'd just wanted to make sure the offer to bunk at her place was still good.

He could easily have found a room at one of the Quarter's many bed-and-breakfasts. Or even at a hotel. Thing of it was, he liked the idea of sticking close to Perry. A sort of sticking that had nothing to do with what her aunt did or did not know about him or his case or his background, and had everything to do with that kiss.

He climbed down from his Yukon, grabbed his duffel bag from the back seat and headed for her door. He was curious to see if she'd decked out her home to look like Sugar Blues, with all its crystals, candles and statues of fairies that looked as if they should be baking cookies in an oven inside a tree.

The key in the lock, he pushed her door and let it swing open while he stood in the entrance taking it all in. He should've known. No beads or Buddha figurines for this woman.

Scarves draped over lampshades turned the walls into a rainbow. He could barely see her sofa, buried as it was beneath a mountain of pillows. And there wasn't an inch of wall not covered with art prints and posters.

"Jack, oh," Perry yelped from the hallway door, drawing his gaze that way. "I wasn't expecting you yet."

Obviously. She wasn't wearing anything but a towel. He reached for the doorknob. "I'll come back later."

"No, wait." She reached out, halting him with the hand not holding the towel to her chest. "I was going to put on the kettle for tea. Let me dress. I'll be right back. Don't go anywhere."

Nodding, he dropped his duffel bag at his feet. "Sure. I'll wait."

The look that came over her face, the light that sparkled in the dark centers of her eyes, her smile that spread until her cheeks plumped like red apples, all of it should have warned him away.

Instead, he headed into the kitchen, filled her tea-kettle from the spigot on the refrigerator door and set it on the stove while he waited.

She was back in minutes, toweling water from her

hair and wearing a black T-shirt and a skirt with more colors than he could count. Not surprisingly, her feet were bare.

"Sorry about that. I came home to nap while Kachina handled the shop. But I couldn't sleep—" she shrugged, tossed the towel to the countertop and shook out her hair "—and I thought a shower might help."

He wasn't certain if she meant it would help her sleep or help her stay awake. He wasn't certain what to say because he hadn't expected to find her here, and because she smelled so damn good. Like oils and incense. "I can leave, or just get a hotel room."

"No. Stay here, please. I like the idea of the place not being empty." The teakettle whistled, and she glanced over, the smile returning. "Thanks. Do you want a cup?"

"Sure," he said, moving aside as she took over the small kitchen.

She lifted the kettle from the heat, and quickly grabbed two mugs from the cupboard and teabags from the pantry. Steam rose when she poured the water, deepening the color on her face. He leaned against the counter behind him, hooked his palms over the edge and watched her.

"How did things go with the reporter?" she asked as she emptied the kettle and returned it to the stove.

He shrugged. "Not so good."

"You didn't learn anything you can use?"

"The only thing I learned is that she doesn't have time to give. Only to receive."

"How so?"

"She's got a great information flow going. All of it incoming. I'm lucky I got the time of day."

"Well, that sucks," Perry said, spooning sugar into her mug, offering him the same. He nodded, and she stirred before handing his mug to him. "What are you going to do now?"

"Do you have an Internet connection? Or a phone jack I can use to dial up?"

"I have cable, and this place is wired like you wouldn't believe. The previous owners were connectivity freaks." She pointed toward the main room. "You can set up on the desk in the living room, or on the dining room table. Either one."

"Great. What about a subscription to the *Times-Picayune?* I want to dig through the archives and see if our reporter ever wrote anything on Eckton Computing or on Dayton Eckhardt before his move to Texas."

"Here's my login," she said, jotting the information onto a notepad hanging on the fridge. "And I'll be out of your way—" the ringing of the phone cut her off, and she smiled "—as soon as I get that."

Jack left his mug on the counter, returned to the front door for the laptop case packed inside his duffel bag. He decided the dining room light would be best, and started setting the computer up on the table.

He could hear Perry's, "Sure. No, it's not a problem. I'll see you tomorrow," coming from the kitchen. And since his was the business of snooping, he listened without remorse to her side of the conversation, curious about *what* wasn't a problem, and who it was she'd be seeing.

She walked into the dining room a few minutes later, bringing him the tea he'd left in the other room. He took the mug from her hand as she settled into the chair opposite the one he'd chosen. He watched her sip at her drink; she did so nervously, flexing her fingers around the mug, refusing to meet his gaze.

"What's up?" he finally asked, when he realized she wasn't going to come clean on her own.

She toyed with the charm at her neck. "That was Della."

"She feeling okay?"

Perry nodded. "She's fine. Better than fine, actually."

"How so?"

"It's Book's night off. He's going to stay over and take care of her."

Ah. He'd wondered about that. "So you don't have to."

"I don't think that's the reason he's staying, but no, I don't have to go back."

"Which means I should pack up and see about that hotel."

"Not necessarily."

He didn't say anything. Just lifted his drink and waited for her to offer him exactly what he wanted.

"You're already set up here," she finally said, waving her hand toward his laptop. "And I've actually spent a lot of nights on the couch. If it's not too short, you're welcome to use it. Or I can sleep there, and you can have the bed."

"I don't have to stay, Perry. Have duffel bag, will

travel, and all that. I can plug in at a coffeehouse and, if I can't find a place, bunk in the back of the Yukon." He'd done it often enough that it wasn't even a hassle. "It's not a problem. Trust me."

"I do trust you. And I'd rather you stayed here with me."

6

DELLA LET her hand rest on the receiver now cradled in its base, pleased that both of her calls had turned out so well. The timing had been iffy on the first; she wasn't sure, when she finally tried to reach Book, if it would be too late to put her plan into motion.

When she'd heard Jack enter the shop to pick up Perry's key from Kachina, Della had made her move. Still at his desk in operations, Book verified that he was off work the next day. Her only moment of panic had come after asking him if he'd like to spend the evening with her. At home. Alone.

His silence had gone on too long. She'd listened to the void, finally hearing him clear his throat and breathe before accepting. They'd talked for a few minutes more, and he'd agreed to stop by around seven. He'd even offered to pick up Chinese, a typically thoughtful gesture. She'd thanked him, certain that nerves would keep her from eating a single bite.

Months ago, she'd given him a key to the front door of the shop as a safeguard, should Perry ever be out of touch. Tonight, the key would come in handy. He could let himself in, and she could stay off her foot. Things couldn't be coming together any better than if she'd plotted this evening for weeks.

Her conversation with Book had given Jack time to make the short drive to Court du Chaud. She'd waited a bit longer in case he'd run into traffic, made any stops or been otherwise delayed. Then she'd dialed her niece's number and made her case. Perry hadn't minded the change of plans at all, and that made Della smile.

As a rule, she was not a busybody—even as she recognized that was drawing a fine line between truth and fiction, considering her entire livelihood was based on what she knew about other people's affairs. She kept her client information confidential, the same as if she were an attorney or physician.

The difference tonight was that her interference was an effort at making amends.

Hobbling around her sitting room, putting things in order, Della wondered if there had ever been another woman less suited to being a mother. The skills that it took had never been in her repertoire. She wasn't sure when she'd first recognized that raising a family was not a lifestyle that suited her situation, but it ended up making no difference. She'd been twenty-eight when Perry had come to her as a frightened child, lost and alone, and nothing else had mattered.

They'd made their way together, Della following to the letter her late brother's instructions for his daughter's rearing, instead of relying on instincts that had never let her down. She hadn't paid any heed to Perry's wishes to be like the other kids.

The result, all these years later, was that they were both products of circumstances into which they'd been thrown, rather than the individuals, the women, they would have become had their lives not been so inexorably intertwined.

It was an interesting look at the human condition, wondering what path each would have chosen had tragic events not determined their way. Her only regret was how insular their world had become as she'd looked after Perry, and Perry, in turn, had looked after her.

And, foolish or not, Della had always put her niece's needs above her own. Which was why she hadn't yet allowed herself to admit her feelings to Book Franklin.

She'd always told herself that if Perry were settled, if Perry didn't depend on her, if Perry this and that, if Perry a dozen different things, then exploring a relationship with Book would be an option.

The truth was that, at forty-eight years old, she didn't know where to begin. Because somewhere along the line, the dynamics had changed. Now Perry was the one doing the looking after, a reality Della had come face-to-face with today. Into Perry's life had walked the amazing Jack Montgomery, and what did Perry do but throw up a protective wall to keep him away.

As weak as Della had been feeling the last few days, from the migraines brought on by her visions, she appreciated the buffer her niece created for her between Sugar Blues and the world.

What she didn't like was how Perry hid behind the wall as well. Which was why, when presented with the opportunity to play interfering, busybody matchmaker, Della had jumped at the chance. Now all she could do was hope her manipulative ways didn't come back to haunt her.

Hearing the bell chime on the door as Book let himself in, Della hopped and limped back to the chaise lounge where she'd already spent too many hours. The aroma of the food he'd brought with him wafted ahead and made her realize that she was hungry after all.

But then, the empty sensation deepened, tightened. And none of what she was feeling had a thing to do with the food. It was a sense of anticipation she'd not let herself experience in years; a hope, a flutter of girlish excitement. And it hit her the moment he walked through the door that she'd loved him for a very long time.

He still wore his suit coat, though his shirt collar was unbuttoned and the knot of his tie hung loose. He'd wrapped one arm around the paper bag he carried, almost like he was charging ahead with a football.

It made her smile, the way he was so unequivocally male, the way her heart raced when she noticed. She laced her fingers tightly together in her lap and watched him come into the sitting room from the landing, well aware of the tension created by her invitation.

"That smells wonderful," she said, hoping to put them both at ease. "I didn't realize how hungry I was till you got here."

"Good. Because I brought more than plenty." He unloaded the containers onto the coffee table, surprising her with a six-pack of beer, then sliding the table closer to the chaise lounge and handing her a pair of chopsticks. Only then did he look around for a place to sit.

"Here. I'll make room." She shifted her legs to the side of the seat, and then she waited, her pulse accelerating, a sheen of perspiration breaking out between her breasts.

He hesitated, and she wasn't sure of the cause until he said, "Do you need anything from the kitchen? Something other than beer? Do you want a glass? Do you need a fork or a knife?"

"I'm fine," she said, still nervously waiting. "Book, I don't bite."

"It's not you I'm worried about," he said under his breath, causing her to wonder if he knew he'd spoken aloud.

But he did sit, and the world didn't come to an end when his hips made contact with her legs. He pulled a bottle from the six-pack, twisted off the top and handed it to her.

Their fingers met when she took it from his hand, the bottle cold, his skin warm. She reacted strongly, a sharp shiver that caught her unawares. He held her gaze for a very long time before bringing his own bottle to his mouth and turning away to drink.

Della drank, too, hoping the buzz from the alcohol would ease what she was feeling, would soften the tension into something sweet. Right now it was unbearable, and she didn't want anything about her time with Book to be that way.

"So, what did you bring me to eat?" she asked, setting her drink on the corner table at her shoulder and snapping her chopsticks together.

Book opened the closest carton. "Spring rolls." Opened another. "Sesame chicken." Opened a third. "Mongolian beef." Opened a fourth. "Kung Pao shrimp."

She leaned forward, clipped a spring roll with her chopsticks and sat back. "You know these things are my favorite foods in the world."

Book chose the beef. "I seem to remember that. The last time we ate dinner together it was Chinese. You and the spring rolls were inseparable."

"My weakness," she said, sighing before biting down. "Mmm. I don't know what it is, but I think I could live on these."

"When was the last time you had them?"

She had to stop and think. "I believe it was the last time you brought them to me."

"Sounds like it's absence making the stomach grow fonder."

She laughed. "Or it's the company that makes everything taste so good."

Book chuckled, dug through the beef and came up with a sliver of bok choy. "If I didn't know you as well as I do, Della Brazille, I'd think you were flirting with me."

She considered him over her bottle of beer. "Would that be a bad thing? If I were?"

He stopped chewing. He stopped picking through the meat and the vegetables. He stopped moving altogether, for a time that seemed longer than she was able to wait.

Finally, he set the carton of food on the table, his chopsticks sticking up like a television antenna, and cocked one knee as he shifted on the seat to face her.

She started counting the beats of his pulse at his temple, but lost track long before he spoke. "What are you asking me, Della?" He shook his head to delay her answer. "I mean, I heard you. I just don't know how honest you want me to be."

She closed her eyes because she already had her answer. She'd heard it in his words, in the tone he'd used when he'd spoken. But she'd seen it even more clearly in his expression, something she was certain he'd meant to hide.

Her gift was both a blessing and a curse. And right now, as in the kitchen earlier with Jack, she wished she was blind to the energy she was picking up from Book.

"It's strange, isn't it?" she asked, opening her eyes again and taking him in. "How long we've known each other. The horrors we've shared. Yet we've never really been honest as a woman and a man."

He hunched forward, his shoulders straining the fabric of his suit coat, and spread his hand on the seat cushion next to her leg, giving her the choice, to touch him, or not to touch him.

"Is that what you want?" He flexed his fingers in the fabric. "Do you want me to tell you the truth? To admit how much you mean to me?"

She placed her drink on the table at her side and straightened, covering his hand, wrapping her fingers around his, then reaching up to caress his cheek. She didn't say a word. All she did was touch him, feel him, sense him.

And then he shook his head, a sly smile crossing his mouth. He turned his palm up and laced his fingers through hers. "I don't have to tell you anything, do I? You already know."

"I know, yes," she admitted, hearing his breath catch, his pulse pound harder and faster. "That doesn't mean I wouldn't like to hear it, anyway. It's been a long time since I've had a man declare his feelings to me."

He brought her hand to his mouth and pressed his lips to the center of her palm. She couldn't even begin to describe the winds of change sweeping through her.

"I've never been very good at expressing myself with words," he admitted, his voice tight, his tone gruff.

Oh, but her heart was filled to the brim and on the verge of bursting. "That's hard to believe, when you have such a very nice mouth."

He arched a brow. "Then let me use it to show you how I feel."

PERRY WOKE with a jolt, uncertain what had startled her from sleep, feeling as if she were in an unfamiliar place when she knew that she wasn't. She was sleeping in her bed. In her room. In her own home, surrounded by all of her things. And then she remembered.

The thing that was different was Jack.

When she'd told him she wanted him to stay the night, he hadn't reacted. At least not in the ways her limited experience with men had taught her to expect. He didn't leer or make any sort of off-color remark about getting lucky.

He'd just shrugged, nodded and continued to hook up his equipment with no more than an agreeable, "Sure."

She'd figured that feeding him would be the hospitable thing to do. Unfortunately, she wasn't much of a cook. If she didn't have salad fixings on hand or leftover containers of takeout, she usually did no more for herself than open a can of soup or make a turkey sandwich. Turkey and soup she had. The deli was her friend.

But the occasion had seemed to call for more effort. After all, Jack was the first man to sleep over since she'd purchased the town house. Not that he was sleeping with her, but he was company. And he had gone out of his way to take care of the repairs to Della's kitchen door.

So she'd boiled pasta, opened and heated a jar of gourmet marinara sauce and grated fresh parmesan over the top. He'd thanked her and dug in, but hadn't been much for conversation, intent instead on his research.

His focus had given her time to study him while eating in silence. Study, and wonder about the man he was. A man who would come into the lives of two women who were strangers, and make himself indispensable in less than two days.

Several minutes into their hushed meal, he'd reached into his laptop case for a pair of reading glasses, grimacing when she'd grinned at him putting them on.

She couldn't help it. He'd looked so…scholarly, so Indiana Jones, what with the touch of gray at his temple, frowning at his screen as he read and jotting illegible notes onto a yellow legal pad. But then she'd taken in the rest of him and realized what a contradiction he was.

She'd been at work when he'd cleaned up and changed in Della's little-used first floor shower. He still wore his Reeboks, today with a pair of black jeans, and instead of yesterday's hoodie, he'd warded off the cold with a bomber jacket over nothing heavier than a T-shirt.

It was that T-shirt that had finally gotten to her. He'd sat there beneath the dining room's low-hanging light fixture, reading, eating, taking notes, his movements economical and concise, but still drawing her gaze.

She'd watched the flexing of his biceps beneath the tight cotton sleeves, watched the binding of the fabric over the balls of his shoulders and the pull over his chest when he stretched.

She'd seen it all earlier when he'd been working on Della's door, but she hadn't been this close, and it hadn't been dark, and they hadn't been alone. Looking away and focusing on her food had put a huge strain on her minimal willpower.

She'd been too aware of having him there. Of what a calming presence he was. Of how easily he'd made himself at home.

Not once in her life had she felt the need to have a man around to provide security or a sense of safety, or to make her complete. But Jack being there, just…being there, had seemed right in more ways than she had fingers to count.

He'd come out of nowhere, bulldozed into her life with a hailstorm of demands, then turned around and in the next breath was so much a part of her existence she didn't remember what the day before had been like without him around. And it was that realization as much as exhaustion that had finally sent her to her room.

In much the same way it had her jolting awake now.

She swung her legs over the side of the bed and eased to her feet. She'd slept deeply, though not long. The bedside clock read 1:00 a.m., and she'd climbed between the sheets at ten.

After a bathroom stop—one that included brushing her teeth and a quick fluff of her bed-head hair—she made her way down the hall, pausing at the living room door.

The main room was dark, but the light was still on in the dining nook. And Jack still sat at the table, jotting notes, glasses perched on the end of his nose.

"Hi," she said, as she walked up behind him and circled the table, sitting in the same chair as before. "Any progress?"

For several seconds, he stared at her over the rims of his glasses, his eyes red, his exhaustion evident. Then he took them off and tossed them onto the table. "What time is it?"

He had a clock on his computer, so surely he knew. "A little after one," she answered, watching as he scrubbed both hands down his face. "Why are you still up?"

He laughed, the sound more snort than chuckle, and seemingly directed at himself. "You stay up long enough, you forget you're supposed to sleep."

She remembered finding him awake in the kitchen almost twenty-four hours earlier. "You didn't sleep at all last night, did you?"

Leaning back in his chair, his hands covering his face, he shook his head. "Maybe thirty minutes. And I drove in from Austin that morning."

"So you've been without sleep for—" she glanced up at the wall clock, too tired to calculate the time "—how long now?"

"God, I have no idea." He sat forward then, forearms on the table's edge, taking her in with a gaze that was too sharply wired for a man as exhausted as he was. "I have a bad habit of not sleeping when I need to."

She laced her hands together on the table. "I think you need to very soon."

"I know." He picked up his pencil, bounced the eraser end on the corner of his laptop. "I've been thinking for a while about hitting the couch."

"But you haven't, because…?"

He shrugged, ran his fingers up and down the pencil's length. "I kept thinking I'd find a connection between Dawn Taylor and Dayton Eckhardt."

Nerves fluttered in Perry's stomach. "So you did find something."

This time when Jack looked up, his excitement snagged her gaze and held. "Her husband used to work for Eckton Computing."

"And?"

"When he couldn't find work after Eckton left New Orleans, he took a short walk off the Causeway Bridge and killed himself."

7

"Do you think Dawn's involved in the kidnapping?" Perry asked as Jack returned to the table.

His announcement of Taylor's suicide had left Perry momentarily lost in thought. He'd used the time to carry his cup and the empty coffee carafe back to the kitchen.

After Perry had cleared their dinner dishes and gone to bed, he'd started nodding off. A combination of exhaustion and pasta. Without a mega dose of caffeine, he'd known there was no way he'd make it through even an hour of his online fact-finding mission.

And as much as he was enjoying Perry's company, as much as he'd like to enjoy even more, she wasn't the reason he was here. He couldn't let go of his focus, couldn't let himself lose sight of his priorities or his purpose.

The Eckhardt family had placed their trust in him, their faith. Their hope that he'd be able to succeed where law enforcement had failed.

They knew his reputation for finding the people he was hired to find. What they didn't know was the road he'd traveled from special ops to private investigation.

"That I'm not sure about," he said, answering Perry's question as he settled back into his seat. "But I am certain that she's not the least bit unhappy that he's missing."

"Wonder what she'd think about him being dead," Perry said, reminding him of Della's last vision of Dayton Eckhardt.

Jack wasn't ready to go there. Not now. Not yet. "I have to operate on the assumption that he's alive and at least marginally well."

"I didn't think you'd do anything else."

He looked up in time to catch her hiding a smile behind her fingertips. "What's that supposed to mean?" he asked.

"The obvious." She fluttered the hand she'd had at her mouth, wrapped her other arm around her middle. "You're a 'just-the-facts' kind of guy. You have to see for yourself before you'll believe. And even then I'm guessing you need to get your hands on whatever it is before you're one-hundred percent convinced."

She'd pegged him pretty damn well. "Some people talk with their hands. I think with mine."

"Then it shouldn't be too hard for you to understand that there are times Della can see things with hers."

Yeah, right. He wasn't going there, either.

"If you'd rather not talk about it, I'll understand. But I am curious." She returned her laced hands to the tabletop. "And eventually, I'll get Della to tell me."

"Tell you what?" Jack asked, fighting the fist that had slammed into his stomach.

"What she saw when she touched you," Perry said,

meeting his gaze, refusing to look away when he glared.

He did not want Perry knowing about his failures, or about the mess he'd made of his life. "Don't psychics have a code of ethics? A doctor-patient confidentiality thing?"

"Whatever goes on between Della and her clients during a reading remains private, yes."

"What happens in Vegas, stays in Vegas?" he mused, not liking the bit of smugness in her smile.

"That's a workable analogy." She lifted a brow. "Except it only applies when it comes to closed sessions."

"Making the rest of us open books, whether we like it or not." He didn't like it. He didn't like it at all.

"Well…" she said, then let the thought trail.

"Go ahead. Enjoy a big fat laugh at my expense." He flicked his pencil across the table. "I'll be gone soon, anyway."

At that, she looked away, picking at a mark on the wooden surface of the table with her thumbnail. "When do you think you'll be leaving?"

"I don't know. Look, I'm sorry. I'm beat, and if this lead with Taylor doesn't pan out I'm stuck with nothing else tangible to go on."

Not to mention that his wanting to get to know her wasn't going so well. Wrong time, wrong place, and all that. Though right now, he wouldn't say no if she offered.

"Is there anything I can do to help?" she asked. "Anything I can look up or print out, or local numbers you need?"

Actually, he had an idea—one that went against his

grain. But with the chips down and the weirdness of the last two days starting to make a twisted sort of sense, he wasn't above looking like a fool if doing so resulted in answers.

So he started to tell Perry everything. But when he focused again on her face, her expression had him forgetting what he was going to say.

Her dark eyes were wide, the brows above raised while she waited for him to answer. She'd washed away what little makeup she'd been wearing before. And as much as he liked the natural look, what he really liked was that she let him see her face.

The beaded earrings that seemed her trademark no longer dangled the length of her neck. She'd pushed her froth of curls behind her ears, and for the first time he noticed the jewels piercing the upper shell. Garnets, he thought, not really up on his semiprecious stones.

She was wearing a tank top that matched her pajama bottoms, so he figured it was a set. A soft looking purple fabric, like that of a well-worn T-shirt. He wished she'd tug it over her head and off.

"Jack?" she prodded, reaching over and touching his wrist.

He looked down to where their skin made contact, hers cool against his, which he couldn't imagine felt anything but hot. And then he lifted his gaze, curious, willing to take a long walk on a short plank if it would get him the truth.

"What do you see?"

She frowned. "Besides the whites of your eyes, which look like road maps?"

"Yeah. How much of your aunt's gift did you inherit?" he asked, not certain he wanted to know if she could see the same things.

She shook her head. "None. I don't know what she saw. All I can see is you."

He wanted to believe her. He couldn't think of what she'd have to gain by lying. Even her efforts to convince him that the trick of the light he'd seen in the stairwell was some sort of spectral energy didn't seem particularly self-serving.

He took a deep breath, and an even deeper leap of faith. "Good. I don't like everyone and his brother knowing where I've been."

She pressed her lips together in that prissy way she had. "So, you think of me as everyone's brother?"

He waited a moment, letting the seconds tick by as the skin in the hollow of her throat grew damp. "No. I don't."

"But you still don't want me to know."

He shook his head.

"Why?"

"Because I don't want you to turn me down when I ask you to come over here and sit on my lap."

PERRY DIDN'T THINK any man had ever said anything to her that made her knees so unbelievably weak, or her heart rush like the wind.

She knew without thinking that things between them would never be the same after this. There was something about Jack she couldn't resist, and she was so very glad to have met him.

It was forever before she remembered to breathe.

Even longer before she managed a response. First, she had to swallow the tight ball of butterflies that had risen on a whoosh of air from her belly up her throat.

And then, what she said was probably not at all what Jack expected to hear. She wasn't even certain if she was ready for what her words implied. All she knew was that trusting her instincts had always been the right choice. She did that very thing now.

"I can't turn you down if you don't ask," she said, blowing out the breath she'd been keeping inside and squeezing his wrist where her fingers still rested. She watched his eyes then, waiting for him to react.

When he did, it was to turn his hand over and force her to make the next move. Oh, but he was sneaky, this one, asking her without speaking, putting the decision into her hands by putting hers into his.

She didn't do it right away. She waited; she made him wait, keeping her fingers on his wrist where she could feel his pulse racing.

"What happens next?" she finally asked, fighting a smile when his mouth twitched.

"Well, if you wait too long, I imagine I'll topple over and spend the night sleeping on the floor."

She rolled her eyes, started to pull her hand away, but then let the tips of her fingers walk over the heel of his palm. "If you're that tired—"

"I'm never that tired," he cut her off to insist, closing her fingers in his fist. "In fact, I'm feeling powerfully wide awake."

"Hmm." She tugged, but he held her tight. "Must be all that coffee."

"It's a second wind."

"Considering how little sleep you've had, it's more likely your third or fourth."

"Then you'd better take advantage of my offer before I expire," he said, appearing on the verge of passing out as he did.

"What exactly were the terms?" she asked, fighting a yawn herself. "I don't remember."

He let her go then, and sat back. "Damn, but you make it hard on a man."

He seemed so miserable, fighting both exhaustion and the losing battle of wits and wills. "How would you feel about a compromise?" she asked.

"What are *your* terms?"

She closed her eyes, found her strength, opened them. "If you come to bed with me now to sleep, I'll sit on your lap in the morning."

"Come to bed with you," he repeated, adding, "to sleep," as if he wasn't quite sure.

Nodding, she got to her feet. "Exactly. And my offer expires with the first step I take away from the table."

"You drive a hard bargain, Ms. Brazille," he said, his voice one notch above a slur. "But I'll take you up on it. Because having you on my lap is something I'd like to be awake for."

He left his glasses and pencil and laptop where they were, and held her hand while he followed her down the hall. Her bedroom was dark. She'd used the bathroom light earlier to guide her way.

It served the same purpose now, allowing them to avoid running into her dresser or her armoire or the spindles at the foot of her four poster bed. She took one side. Jack took the other.

Since she was already in her pajamas, all there was for her to do was crawl between the sheets. But she waited, because she didn't want to miss a second of watching him take off his clothes.

He held on to the footboard for balance as he toed off his shoes, reached down to tug off his socks. His T-shirt was next. He whipped it over his head and off, and she was left standing there, looking at black denim and bare skin.

She wanted to flip on the light because really, how fair was it that she could see so little of him after being tempted for two days by his T-shirts?

When his hands went to the fly of his jeans, her breath caught, and she forced herself to climb onto the mattress. Sitting with her legs tucked beneath her, she pulled the blankets to her chin and listened to the flip of the brass buttons through the holes of his fly.

And then his jeans came down in a scratch of denim over skin, and she saw the dark fabric of boxers before she felt the dip of the mattress beneath his weight.

He was warm beside her, and his heat was as comforting as his smell. He reminded her of the big outdoors, the freshness of rain, the snap of the cold that had hit them in January after December's unusual dog days.

He dropped to his back, tugged the blankets to his chest, rested an arm over his eyes. He didn't say a word, and it wasn't three minutes before his breathing was deep and even.

She sighed, scooted down and rolled to her side, her back to him as she faced the wall. She fought a twinge of disappointment that sharing a bed with her wasn't enough to keep him awake.

But then logic took over. The man hadn't slept in days. She doubted he could stay awake for any woman at this point. Well, maybe Carmen Electra. Or Angelina Jolie.

In the next moment, before she could come up with another well-endowed name, he rolled toward her. Draping an arm over her waist, he cuddled up against her, pressing the spoon of his body to hers.

When he began snoring lightly in her ear, she realized how deeply asleep he'd fallen. He was so wonderfully close, so soothingly warm, so large and so comfortably…there, just there, that she found herself drifting off, content and relaxed beneath the weight of his arm.

It was the movement of that arm that roused her. Her lashes fluttered. She blinked, glanced over her shoulder at the red dotted numbers on the face of her clock. They'd been asleep for less than thirty minutes. And it was obvious that Jack wasn't sleeping now.

He was breathing in her ear, shallow breaths, choppy breaths, all the while quietly working his hand beneath her top to her skin. Once he got past the fabric, once his palm lay flat on her belly, once his fingertips grazed the lower swells of her breasts, he grew still.

And for several long seconds, he stayed that way.

She, on the other hand, grew itchy and tight. Her nipples hardened. Her skin flushed. She contracted the muscles deep inside her sex, and slipped a hand between her legs to ease the tension.

He chuckled. "Wasn't sure you were ever going to wake up."

Humph. "If you've been trying for a while, then you haven't been trying very hard."

"I'm not in any hurry. Besides, you were enjoying your beauty sleep."

Beauty sleep? "What's that supposed to mean?"

"You purr like a kitten when you snore."

She supposed that wasn't a bad thing. If she snored. Which she didn't.

"Kinda makes me wonder what other animal noises you make," he said.

"Well, let's see," she said, rolling slowly onto her back and taking care not to dislodge his hand. She liked the weight of it, the calluses, the warmth, as much as she liked his need to touch. "I can snap like a turtle."

He laughed. "That one doesn't surprise me."

His noticing that aspect of her personality didn't come as a surprise to her, either. "I can growl like a mama lion, or coo like a dove."

"Those work," he said, cuddling closer, weighting her down with a knee on her thigh. "If you want to demonstrate, I'm all ears."

No, what he was was all hard body. His arm, his chest, his leg. And then there was the other hardness pressing into her hip. The one reminding her she hadn't done this in a very long time. The one she couldn't ignore.

"I don't perform on command." She drew up her knees, knocking his leg back to the bed. "I need…inspiration. Or the promise of a reward."

"What if I give you both?" he asked, his voice dropping to a husky growl.

She wanted him in ways that frightened her. She'd never known this overwhelming physical need. And she couldn't help but wonder if what she was feeling went beyond wanting what he could do to her body.

She turned her head on the pillow, seeing little beyond the form of his head, and a tiny light she thought might be his eyes. Her voice shook when she said, "Actually, I'd like that more than you can imagine."

He leaned over then and kissed her. Just touched his mouth to the corner of hers, left it there and breathed deeply, doing nothing else.

The hair on his chest tickled her shoulder, but the contact was nowhere close to being enough. She wanted more. She wanted everything. She just didn't know where to start.

As if reading her mind, he pulled her up to a sitting position, taking over the way she wanted. He peeled off her tank top, leaning against her when she lay back down, brushing her breasts with his chest's soft hair, pressing himself close. His pecs were firm, his stomach solid.

His T-shirt had teased her, hinting at but never revealing his body's truth. He was fit, his skin smooth, his flesh resilient. She ran her palms over his shoulders and down his back, slipped her fingers beneath the waistband of his boxers and teased him there.

"If those are in your way, I'll be glad to take them off," he said, chuckling deep in his chest.

The vibrations tickled, and she smiled. "I'll let you know when they get to be a problem."

"Are you sure they're not a problem now?"

Men. So predictable. But with this one she wouldn't change a thing, she mused, pulling her hands from his waistband to trace her way up his spine. She fingered the scar she found on his shoulder blade, a deep crescent carved into his skin, but stayed silent when he stiffened at her touch.

He slid lower on her body, kissing the valley between her breasts, stopping just above her navel to ask, "You don't mind if I get rid of yours, do you? They're definitely in my way."

She nodded. She shook her head. She wasn't sure which answer was the one he wanted, or even what she was trying to say. But when his hands gripped the fabric, she stopped thinking and willingly let him strip her bare.

"Mmm," he murmured, back to kissing her now. "I like the way you smell."

She closed her eyes, flexed her fingers into the sheet at her hips. She didn't know if he was talking about her soap or her perfume or the scent of her arousal, so she didn't respond. Except that wasn't exactly true.

Her hips came up off the bed, and her legs opened. She wanted him there desperately and was ready to beg, but he settled between her thighs before she had to, and kissed his way from her belly to her sex. His tongue was wet and warm, and she shivered.

His hands were broad where he slipped them beneath her hips and squeezed. When he drew her clit between his lips, she gasped, shuddered and moaned from the exquisite sensation. She felt herself open, felt herself weep as her body grew ready to take him.

He slid a finger inside her, added another, pushed deep while he slicked his tongue through her folds. He stroked, his fingers moving in and out. He sucked, the pressure of his lips light, the swirling teasing tip of his tongue an elegant torture.

It was too much, and it had been so long, and she cried out, letting go. Spasms ripped through her, a sweet singing bliss, a release that swept through her like a flood after rain. He stayed with her all the way, fingering, kissing, pressing against her as she came.

And then it was over. She was done, boneless and weak, exhausted and spent. Her body finished thrumming, the burning eased, and she settled into the mattress like a big fat cat taking a nap, barely aware of Jack settling in beside her as she slept.

8

THE NEXT TIME she opened her eyes it was eight o'clock. She wasn't due at work until ten. For the first time in her memory, she considered calling in sick.

She wouldn't, of course. And she wasn't. Unless too little sleep and an orgasmic hangover counted.

She groaned as the guilt hit her, feeling the heat of a blush turn her skin what she knew would be a bright, splotchy red. She had fallen asleep on him. She, the female. A humiliating reversal of fortunes.

Hiding in the closet until he left ranked at the top of her list of escape routes. But first she wanted to know about the scar on his back—where it had come from, how long he'd had it, why he'd turned to stone when she'd discovered it there.

She knew nothing about who he was beyond his being an investigator from Texas. She wanted to know more. She wanted to know everything.

Lying on her stomach and not wanting Jack to wake, she turned just her head—only to find that he wasn't sleeping. And that he was looking at her.

"Hi," she said.

"Good morning," he responded.

"I'm sorry. About last night. Er, about earlier. I went to sleep."

"So did I."

His lashes were so long it killed her. She rolled onto her side to face him. "I know. But I got…you didn't…"

"Don't worry about it," he said, understanding what she was trying to say, and also picking up on her angst. "No man ever died from a broken hard-on."

She couldn't decide whether to smile or grimace, and ended up doing a bit of both. "That was horrible."

"I know. A girl I knew in high school used to say it all the time." He reached up and tucked her hair behind her ear; his touch caused her to shiver. "She hung with me and three other guys, and got sick of hearing us complain about being left high and dry."

"I don't blame her," she said, sliding her feet between his. "And besides, she was right."

"She was right about a lot of things," he said with a self-deprecating snort.

Interesting—both how he could appreciate a teenage girl's insight, and his own conceit. "You were close to her, then?"

Toying with her hair again, he nodded, his eyes an ever-deepening gray. "She was like family. Hell, she was family."

"How so?" she asked, wondering how long it would take him to cut off her prying.

He blew out a deep breath, ran his knuckle over the skin beneath her chin. "During my senior year, I saw more of her and the guys than I did my father."

She heard the slight catch in his voice, was curious

if he'd noticed that his armor had slipped. "Where was he?"

"In and out," he said with a shrug, toying with the swell of her breast. "He was supposed to be in Austin with me, but he spent most of his time in Baltimore with my mother. My sister was sick, and going through a trial program at Johns Hopkins. She died when I was stationed in Kuwait."

"Jack, I'm so sorry." She reached over, caressed his face.

He captured her hand, brought it to his chest and held it there. "Don't be. It was a long time ago. Hell, sixteen years. It's over."

She knew better. She'd lived through a similar blow. Nothing like that was ever over. She threaded her fingers through the hair on his chest and tugged. "Is that where you got the scar? The one on your shoulder? In Kuwait?"

He took so long to answer that she feared she'd hit a nerve still wounded and raw. But then he said, "Actually, no. I was in international waters for that one."

"Oh." Lame, but it was all she could think of to say. "I'm sorry."

His chuckle broke the tension. "You know, you've said that three times in the last thirteen minutes."

"No. I didn't know." She glanced over her shoulder at the clock, glanced back. "Are you timing something?"

"Yeah. How long it's going to take you to find the rest of my scars."

She waited…waited…until finally she bit. "That sounds like a challenge to me."

He rolled onto his back, punched a pillow beneath his head, lay propped on his stacked wrists like a king. "I'm all yours."

She pushed up onto her elbow, intrigued by what he was offering her, and nervous at the same time. "You'll tell me about any scars that I find?"

He nodded. "The one on my shoulder's off-limits, but I'll tell you about the rest. In fact—" he found her hand, guided it to a gouge on his side between two ribs "—this is the one from Kuwait."

She dipped her finger into the hollow there, felt the jaggedly healed pocket of skin. "A knife?"

"A shiv, yeah. Hurt like a son of a bitch, and I don't even want to think about where the blade had been." He shuddered; it seemed an involuntary response. "We did what we could with field dressing and a shot of penicillin, but the damn thing took forever to heal."

She wanted to ask more—who had stabbed him, why he'd been in such a position, if he'd caught the bad guy, who he'd included in "we"—but he'd moved her hand lower by then.

Sometime during the night, he'd managed to lose his boxers. His skin was warm, the muscles in his hips well-defined. She swirled her fingers there, where he'd left them, finally discovering the knot of puckered flesh that could only be one thing.

Her heart raced. "A gunshot?"

He nodded. "Chechnya. Uh, '96? The one on my knee came from the Sudan, the year before."

But that was all he said. She sat up, found the gash on his knee, never asking a thing about what he'd been doing in all those places. The damage to his body told her the truth.

Jack Montgomery was a dangerous man. He'd done things, seen things, traveled to places she'd only read about.

Yet here he was, naked and open, and giving without expecting to receive in return. She didn't understand what seemed to be a contradiction. She didn't understand this man, not at all.

She slid her fingers from his knee up his thigh to his hip, the edge of her hand brushing his groin. He sucked in a sharp fizz of breath.

"That thing you promised last night?" he reminded her. "About sitting in my lap?"

She started to nod, found herself frozen.

"This would be a really good time."

She closed her eyes, screwed up her courage, told herself that he wasn't here to hurt her, knowing that if it happened then this was the path she had chosen to take. She leaned forward to kiss him just beneath his heart.

He smelled wonderful, and tasted so good she couldn't help it. She eased lower, feeling his erection bob against her chest as she climbed up and straddled his legs. Once there, she inched lower and took him into her mouth.

He arched up, groaned, held her shoulders while she wrapped her fingers around his shaft and plied her tongue over and around the ripe head of his cock.

She toyed with the slit in the tip, licked her way along the seam beneath, circled the ridge above the ring of her fingers where she held the top of his shaft. He was smooth and salty, and she loved the sounds he made, the deep throaty moans and primal growls.

But then he stopped her, lifting her away, reaching for a condom and putting it on. Then he dragged her up his body so that his sheathed erection throbbed between them, before he kissed her full on the mouth. He gripped her bottom, kneed apart her legs, pushed her up and positioned himself to thrust.

Before he did, however, he paused, pulling free from her mouth to tell her, "As much as I love you having your way, that tongue of yours was about to do me in, and I'd really like this to last more than ten seconds."

She smiled. She couldn't help it. He was so cute and so miserable all at the same time. "Don't get your hopes up. I'm not exactly a paragon of patience."

"So I noticed last night."

He was being such a good sport that she didn't take offense. What she did was plant her hands on his chest and push upright, lowering herself slowly as his cock slid deep and pulsed inside her, as she clenched and squeezed.

For several seconds, she sat there, breathing hard, searching for her control and trying to ignore the way he filled her. An impossible task, of course, and so she began to move.

She dug the heels of her palms into his shoulders, pushing down as she rotated her hips. He held her there, just above her thighs, his fingers digging in as he thrust up to meet her downward strokes.

She laughed. This was breathtaking, being with him, being filled by him. She didn't think she'd ever had it so good; making love meant so much more than just having sex.

"What's so funny?" he fairly growled, grabbing her harder.

"Not funny. Glorious. You feel so amazing." He surged up, captured her nipple and sucked. She hissed back a breath. "And that feels like I'm not going to last."

He let her go and growled, saying, "Good. Because I'm right there with you."

She felt him heat, felt the tightening between her legs, felt the surge of sensation spiraling. She gave in, came apart, cried out as she shuddered, as even her shoulders shook.

He waited until she was done, but just barely. He drove deep, thrust hard; she fell forward onto his chest and rode the wave.

Afterward, he held her close, eventually rolling them both to the side. She needed to get up. She didn't want to get up. With his arms wrapped around her, their bodies still joined, she didn't want to move at all.

She didn't want anything to break the spell of this magic that felt like the heaven of forever.

HAVING HER WAY nearly killed him. Either Jack was more exhausted than even he had realized, or Perry knew every trick in the book about draining him dry. She'd left him five minutes ago, groaning as she climbed from the bed, mumbling something about getting ready for work.

He needed to do the same. To steam the sludge from his brain. To put a call into Cindy Eckhardt and ask her if she was familiar with Dawn Taylor. It wasn't a lot, but it was a start.

He swung up into a sitting position and scrubbed his hands over his face. He pushed to his feet, stumbled over his own freaking shoes, shirt and pants as he headed for the bathroom—and toward the woman who'd just upended his life.

Best he could tell by the morning light sneaking in through Perry's drapes, her bedroom was the same riot of colors and clutter as the living room, dining room and kitchen. And when he pushed open the bathroom door, he got hit with more of the same.

Red and yellow wall tiles, candles, flooring and towels. The space was small and steamy, and it smelled like spices that had nothing to do with a restaurant kitchen or holiday baking, and everything to do with a palace harem in Istanbul. Spices that were heavy and rich, and put him in mind of sex.

Not that his mind had been anywhere else for hours, but he wondered if she chose the scents she did—the candles, the soap, the shampoo—because it put her in mind of the same. Or if it was more a case of her not having a subtle bone in her body.

The colors, the fabrics, the scents, even the earrings she wore, and the way she kissed, and her wild cloud of hair. All of it was big and vibrant and involved, and got his juices flowing.

He shut the door behind him, the sound of the latch clicking loud enough for her to hear above the running water. He didn't want to frighten her, and an invitation wouldn't be a bad thing. Who knew what went on with women and their showers?

He'd barely finished the thought when the frosted door slid open on its tracks and there Perry stood, naked and dripping and a contrast in colors. Her hair hung in wet hanks to the tops of her breasts. It was jet black, the same color as her big bright eyes and the thatch of hair between her legs.

Her skin, on the other hand, was lily white, a delicate porcelain pale, the only color that of the dark cherry centers of her breasts. He'd tasted her, made love to her, had her mouth on him, but there was something about seeing her like this that wound him up hot and tight.

He thought about moving, thought about standing where he was and enjoying the view for as long as he could, ended up licking his lips and laughing when Perry rolled her eyes.

"I want to know something," she said, backing up when he started toward her.

He climbed into the tub, slid the door closed behind him, breathed deeply of the spice and the steam. "What's that?"

"Well, actually, a couple of things."

He put his hands on her shoulders and switched their positions so that he stood under the spray. "I can't answer if you don't ask."

She crossed her arms. "The case. What are you going to do next?"

It was hard to take her interest in his business seriously when they were both naked and wet. "More interviews. Friends of the Taylors. I want to find out what the couple was feeling about Dayton Eckhardt before and after the company's move. Then I'll talk to ex-employees who worked with Taylor specifically."

"Okay. Good." She swiped wet hair out of her eyes. "You'll let me know what I can do to help?"

Yesterday, she didn't want a thing to do with him or his case, and now she counted herself involved. He ducked under the spray to wet his hair, sputtered when he came up for air. "Sure. If that's what you want."

"It is." She nodded vigorously as if making sure she had his attention.

"Well, there is one thing…"

"What?"

It was off the cuff, as were many of his best ideas, but he still wasn't sure he could make it work. "I thought if she's up to it, I'd like to take your aunt to the old Eckton warehouse. See if she might pick up any vibes."

Perry stacked her hands behind her on the wall and leaned against them, her expression less curious than it was smug. "Does that mean you've changed your mind?"

"About?" he said, reaching for her shower gel and sponge.

"Her gift."

He shook his head, admitting to nothing, soaping his armpits and his chest. "It's not that so much as the fact that I'm running low on options."

"Hmm." She canted her head to one side. "I thought it might be about what Della saw when she touched you."

Suds fell from the sponge to his feet. "Who said she saw anything?"

"No one." She paused, screwed her mouth to one side as if the movement helped her concentrate. "It's just that I can't think of any other reason you'd have changed your mind."

"Who said I've changed my mind?" he asked, tossing her the sponge and turning around.

She scrubbed the width of his shoulders, circled her way down his back, across his hips, up his arms. The pressure was perfect, the massage soothing, the sponge soapy soft and damn arousing.

"Why are you so hardheaded?"

"I can get harder."

"Get as hard as you like." She shoved the sponge between his legs, and he jumped. "I think Della did see something. And you not wanting to talk about it is proof."

He turned around before she did any permanent anatomical damage. "Proof that I don't want to talk about it. That's all."

"Why won't you tell me?" She asked the question with such petulance, he expected to see her stomp her feet.

"There's nothing to tell." Though he wondered what would happen if he did tell her, what she would do if he counted up the number of men he'd killed and laid it out—the truth, in stark black and white.

"Is it because you don't trust me?"

"No," he said, steeling himself against her pleas.

"You do or you don't?"

"Doesn't matter." He shook water from his face. "That's not the reason."

Her chin went up. "Then just tell me the truth."

He felt a big, fat Jack Nicholson moment coming on and had to stop himself from blurting out, "You can't handle the truth."

Instead, he said, "I'm not going to tell you because it's none of your business."

That shut her up. Or so he thought, until she said, "She did see something, didn't she?"

"Perry, do me a favor." He jerked the sponge from her hand, tossed it to the floor of the tub behind him. "Let it go. Just let it go."

He didn't want her to know any more than he'd told her about the dysfunction that had plagued his biological family. He didn't want her to drag out details of the covert missions that had taken him to Chechnya and to the Sudan.

And he sure as hell didn't want her to find out that the case before Eckhardt's had nearly killed him. That the family who'd hired him to find their daughter had ended up letting him go. That nothing he'd done had brought him close to discovering the six-year-old's fate. That even now, in his downtime, he continued to turn over the same clues again and again and again, thinking of that little girl, her blond curls bouncing, her eyes so bright and blue. Thinking, too, about the predator that might have her, about her parents imagining the worst.

Thinking, most of all, about his inability to give them the closure they sought.

Moisture threatened to well in his eyes. His throat begin to ache like raw meat. He rinsed his face, doused the memories, shook away the ugliness along with the water, before looking down.

Perry considered his demand for several long seconds, weighing her nosiness against his nakedness, her voice trembling a bit when she finally said, "Make me."

It was exactly what he needed. The light in her eyes. The breathlessness in her words. The invitation to lose himself in her body.

"My pleasure," was his only response, before he bent to kiss her.

He laced their fingers together, held their hands against the wall shoulder high, and refused to let her move. He was done with talking, done with plotting and planning and all this digging around in his psyche, where he didn't let anyone else dig.

She opened her mouth willingly, met his tongue as if she'd been waiting all this time for him to ask. No, not to ask. To take. To do so with her permission, for her enjoyment. Much the way she'd taken him.

It was a kiss of heavy heartbeats and labored breathing. A kiss of high expectations, rampant need and joy. His cock jutted boldly from his body, and he smelled the rising musk of her desire.

He wanted to taste her, to drink her in; he dropped to his knees and held her hips while he buried his face in her belly. Her skin was spicy and sweet and soft, and he nipped at the flesh around her navel.

She threaded her fingers into his hair and groaned, spread her legs to give him access. He took it all, brushing aside her curls and kissing her plump lips.

She was soft and she was swollen, and he parted her with his thumbs to lick through her folds, drawing the hard knot of her clit into his mouth and holding her while she shuddered.

She didn't shudder long. Before she was even finished, he was back on his feet. But when he got there, he wasn't sure what to make of the longing in her expression. He couldn't tell what she wanted. He didn't know what to do.

"Please," she whispered. "I want—"

"What? Anything."

"I know it's silly."

"It's not."

"I'm nervous."

"Don't be."

"It's not that I don't like—"

"Tell me. Show me."

"I don't want—"

"I do. You. Now."

He could hardly speak for how much he wanted her. And in the next moment she blew him away by turning around, bending over, and bracing one foot on the edge of the tub.

He reached for the condom he'd left on the counter and moved in, grabbed her by the hips, dipped his knees and guided his sheathed cock to her entrance. She was ready, and she pushed against him, urging him to meet her halfway.

Water beat against his spine, swirled around his feet. Steam rose to the ceiling. The smells of sex and spices followed. He noticed everything. Noticed all that he could.

He had to. If he didn't get his mind off the reality of his throbbing cock, he was going to come and be of no use to her at all.

He played with her clit, pressing where she showed him to press, rubbing when her fingers asked. And all the while he thrust. Slow strokes. Deadly strokes. Long, even strokes meant to kill a man.

She was so tight and so wet, and he wasn't talking about the water from the shower. He was talking about the way she wanted him, how her body told the truth, and then he couldn't even remember why he was trying to wait.

He groaned. She cried out, shaking and shivering, reaching between her legs to where their bodies were joined and stroking him in turn. The pleasure was almost more than he could bear.

But he didn't want to come this way. He wanted to make this personal. He wanted to leave his mark. He pulled free from her body, waited for her to stand and turned her, backing her into the slick tile wall and hooking her thighs with his hands.

He lifted her, spread her, drove up and into her again. She gasped, gripped his shoulders, held on while he thrust. He kissed her neck, sucked her skin between his lips and nipped, drinking the water that sluiced over her, finally finding her mouth.

He kissed her, his tongue sliding over hers, their

breath mingling as they wheezed and huffed. Her fingers bruised his shoulders. His bruised her thighs. But still he held her, thrusting, pumping, the base of his spine burning with his need to come.

And then it happened. Perry pulled her mouth from his and cried out, "Jack! Oh, Jack. I'm coming apart." He let go, unloading, filling her with all the frustration and pent-up need and sense of loss she demanded.

He gave her his all; he ached with it, fearing that it was too late to stop from giving her his heart.

THEY WRAPPED UP IN matching towels and returned to the bedroom, both beyond exhausted and showing it. Perry could barely walk. For that matter, she was having trouble standing up straight. And all this time she'd thought she was in such good shape.

Then again, sex seemed to be a great equalizer in the fitness department. Jack had collapsed on the bed, his legs spread, his towel parting to show a whole lot of muscled thigh and a teasing hint of the dark hair at his groin.

She couldn't resist, smiling to herself and feeling strangely, wonderfully bold as she reached up and pulled the edges apart, dropping the towel to the bed, baring his scarred body, drinking her fill.

Having never been a voyeur, it surprised her how much she liked looking at him, just looking—at the hair in his armpits, the flat discs of his nipples, the bulge of his triceps, the ripple of his abs, his penis at rest on the thatch of thick hair that also cushioned his balls.

Surprising herself further, she whipped off her towel, liking the way he looked at her, too—even if she was too sore to do anything about it. Not to mention she had to get to work.

He stayed still for several seconds before pushing up onto his elbows and staring at her. Taking her in. Up and down. Over and over until she could no longer breathe.

"It's not going to work, you know," he said, "seducing me into telling you all my deep dark secrets."

"Who said anything about secrets or seducing?" Brow arched, she dropped her gaze lower, to his penis, lying limp between his spread thighs. "Besides, it was working fine five minutes ago."

"Very funny," he grumbled. "You're not taking into account that I'm out of shape."

"Your shape is just fine."

This time he growled. "Out of practice, then, okay? Out of practice."

Hmm. Interesting. Especially the part where he sounded less than pleased for telling her.

She crossed the room and pulled a bra and panty set from her bureau drawer, making an admission she should have already shared. "I'm out of practice, too."

He snorted. "Right."

What was that supposed to mean? "Seriously. It's been, uh…" Gah, did she really want him to know? "Uh, years."

He waited a moment, narrowed his eyes as he watched her dress. "How many?"

"You tell me, I'll tell you."

A brow went up. "Isn't this the conversation we were supposed to have before?"

Men. Always so…manlike. "Better late than never, I always say."

He snickered at that. "Something about a horse and closing a barn door is bothering me here."

Infuriating man. Still, if they were going to take this…this…what they'd done further, she wanted him to know. "All right. It's been six years."

"Hmm. Well. It's been…a while for me."

"A while?" she asked, snapping the elastic of her panties into place.

"Yeah, you know. Here and there." He gave a shrug that didn't come across as quite as careless as she thought he'd intended. "Nothing important. Always protected."

Right now, she didn't have time to process all that his admission—or his attitude—implied. "I suppose we're doubly safe, then."

"You're on the pill?"

She sighed, reached back to hook her bra. "Does it make me seem pathetic that I am? I mean, celibacy's as effective as birth control gets. Why the overkill, you know?"

Jack reached up, punched a pillow beneath his head, cleared his throat before saying, "Because celibacy doesn't take chemistry into account."

Was that all this was? Physical chemistry? Was that really what he thought? "So why nothing long-term for you? Have you been in Tibet?"

He frowned. "Tibet?"

"At a monastery. Or at the South Pole studying penguins and their bad habits?"

One corner of his mouth lifted. "That was bad."

"Really?" she asked, grabbing her towel and squeezing what water she could from her hair. "I thought it amazingly clever."

He shuddered. "Do you have any heat in this place? I'm freezing my balls off here."

She tossed him the duffel bag she'd brought into the room before she'd climbed into the shower. "Guess you didn't get used to the conditions while you were away, Tibet and the South Pole both being so cold and all."

He sat up, covered his lap with the blanket before digging for clean clothes. "I haven't been out of the country since my discharge."

Facts. Good. They were getting somewhere. "When was that?"

"Eight years ago."

She canted her head and considered him. "How old are you?"

"Then, I was thirty."

"I'm thirty now."

"Good. That means you're old enough."

Uh-oh. "For what?"

He paused, paused, and paused another few seconds, then said, "To not think that showering together means anything more than conserving water. Or that sharing a bed is about more than sleeping."

"Actually," she began, working for flippant, feeling

the heat of embarrassment rise, "I've been waiting for you to suggest we start shopping for rings. I'm free today if you are."

Jack sighed. "Think about it. It's been a while for both of us, and we met under pretty strange circumstances."

Fine. Whatever. God, she couldn't breathe. And why was her chest aching? "Oh, hey, don't worry your pretty head about it. Strange circumstances always have me horny and getting naked in the shower."

"Don't do this, Perry."

"Don't do what?"

"Make this into something it's not."

"Then tell me, Jack. What is it?"

"It's sex, Perry. That's all."

She wasn't going to let him hurt her. She wasn't. She wasn't. This wasn't a romance. It wasn't too late to back out.

She was such a liar. Such a liar. Still… "C'mon, Jack. Don't you think I know that without you giving me some shit about conserving water? Like you said, I'm old enough to know what I'm doing."

She was also old enough to march into her walk-in closet and close the door behind her without once looking back. And that's exactly what she did.

9

LYING WITH ONE arm beneath his head, the other draped across his bare stomach, Book Franklin stared up at Della Brazille's bedroom ceiling. He couldn't see much of anything as dark as it was, the only light in the room peeking through a gap in the heavy blue drapes.

The lack of visibility wasn't a big deal. He could only think of one thing—one woman—he wanted to see, and since Della was at his side sleeping, that was good enough.

It wasn't as if, since seeing them last, he'd forgotten anything about the tiny dimple in the hollow of her throat or the patch of freckles on her shoulder or the knot above her ankle from a poorly set break. And the way she'd looked up at him, the tears she'd cried as they'd made love, sure as hell hadn't slipped his mind.

Thinking of everything he'd learned about her during the night had more than his heart aching. The fact that someone wanted to hurt her weighed large on his mind, making sleep impossible. It was time to get up anyway, or would be if he could bring himself to leave her side.

He couldn't. All he could think about was the reality that if she'd been standing three feet closer to the door when that brick had come sailing through, he wouldn't be in bed with her now.

He was still having a hard time believing that after all this time she'd been the one to make the first move. He'd never talked to her about his feelings, figuring there wasn't any need, that more than likely she knew as much about them as he did.

The last two years had been trying, not knowing if she felt the same, if they would continue to see one another only as cop and psychic.

Until last night, he hadn't realized how very much he wanted them to share more than a professional relationship. How waking up to her every morning was about the most perfect life he could imagine. He just couldn't figure how making it happen was possible.

Call him old-fashioned and a chauvinist, but he hated the idea of subjecting the woman he loved to his schedule and his life. The hours were brutal, the situations in which he often found himself even more so.

Sure, he could be driving to an office job and get hit by a tractor trailer, but the odds of not coming home in one piece were a whole lot higher as a member of the NOPD than if he'd belonged to an organization of CPAs.

Then again, maybe he was being a prick about it. He knew plenty of guys who made it happen. He just didn't see himself being one of them. Not after having his own father gunned down in the line of duty.

Book had been fifteen when it had happened. His

mother had never recovered, and he'd been thrust like a big fat cliché into a role he wasn't ready for. How many fifteen-year-olds, whose previous focus had been how to get that baseball scholarship, would be?

The man of the house. What a joke. He'd been the survivor of the house. The level head. The only source of sanity or common sense. It had been a hell of a jump from being a kid intent on playing ball to bearing the weight of the Franklin world on his shoulders.

He didn't want to put Della through anything like that. Or worse, to imagine her suffering the same fate as his mother.

He needed to go see her. It had been way too long since he'd visited her in the nursing home where she'd been living for the past two years. It was hard to see her so frail, so forgetful, most times not even recognizing him.

"Yes. You do," Della whispered at his side.

Damn uncanny woman. "I do what?"

"You need to check in with your mother." That was all she said as she scooted closer, cuddled up to his side, and placed her hand over his. "She might not know you now, but you don't want her to worry about the boy she remembers."

He didn't think he'd ever been so grateful for the dark as he was now, what with the way his face was burning. "How do you do that?"

"I try not to. At least, when it's a situation where my insight hasn't been sought out." She laced her fingers through his. "You were so still and so quiet. I knew you weren't sleeping, and then I picked up a sense of conflict between you and your mother. That mostly she doesn't know you any longer, and that keeps you away."

"It's complicated," he said, then snorted. Complicated wasn't a strong enough word. "Aren't most relationships between parents and kids?"

"I don't think so. Though I imagine you see more than your fair share."

He tightened his grip on her fingers, as if it would keep her close. "Did you ever want kids of your own?"

On the pillow beside him, she shook her head. "I knew a long time ago I wasn't motherhood material."

"Having Perry with you didn't change your mind?"

Della's laughter was as soft as her skin. "Oh, no. I was a horrible parent. Instead of trusting my instincts, I studied how-to guides and followed each and every instruction. Try doing that when every third thing out there contradicts the first two."

"Huh. Seems strange, considering that you can see so much about others."

"It's like the cobbler's own shoes always being in need of repair." The bedcovers rustled as she shifted to lay her head on his shoulder. "Besides, who purposefully seeks out their own faults?"

"Most of us don't need to. We face them on a daily basis."

She was quiet after that, letting several long seconds tick by lost in thought. He wondered if he'd said something wrong. Or if she'd started counting all of his shortcomings and had already lost track.

So when she finally spoke, she caught him off

guard. And what she said set his heart to pumping. "It wasn't your fault that your father was killed. And putting in the hours you do won't bring him back."

He breathed in, waited, breathed out, paused. And then he swung his legs over the side of the bed and sat. "I put in the hours I do because of the scum on the streets. The more I can scrape up, the fewer bricks and broken windows and kidnapped computer gurus to deal with."

Della sat up, moving behind him to massage his shoulders. He couldn't relax, couldn't find the peace of mind to enjoy the soothing touch of her fingers.

He got to his feet before she could "sense" anything else about him, and hunted on the floor for his clothes. The phone rang when he was zipping his pants. Della turned on the bedside lamp and answered.

The conversation was short, and obviously with her niece. He picked up just enough from Della's side to figure out Perry wanted them to meet her somewhere. As long as Della was up to it, he'd welcome the distraction.

He preferred working in the present, focusing on the here and now. The past was long gone; it couldn't be changed—even though he wished every day that it could.

THAT KISS to the neck had been a mistake. It was a kiss she had known would never be enough. It was a kiss that should never have happened.

Drake wanted more. Always more. He couldn't get his fill of her. And getting what she wanted of him had begun to be a problem more than a joy.

Big Bruiser Babin didn't like the idea of his wife making her way home alone. He liked even less her doing so in the company of another man.

Drake had seen her safely away from the club that first night. He'd walked her through the courtyard and up to her own back door.

Big Bruiser had been in the kitchen. He'd seen them walk up. He'd met them on the stoop. He'd been polite to Drake. He'd been a sweet potato dumpling to her.

And then he'd told her he'd be stopping by the Golden Key every night when she sang to take her home himself. He hadn't listened to her objections— he was too busy to have to play nursemaid to her—he'd simply put his foot down.

He'd never cottoned to the idea of leaving her there unchaperoned, but he knew what it meant to her to sing. Being the chief of police allowed Big Bruiser Babin the freedom to do just about anything he wanted to do.

It also meant he never worried about his own coming to harm. He considered himself untouchable, higher than the law he upheld, immune to the misfortune that befell the men whose rehabilitation rested on his broad shoulders.

That particularly arrogant trait had first brought him to Sugar's notice. But it had soon caused her admiration to drift, her affections to drift as well.

After all, when she'd said, "I do," to Big Bruiser, she hadn't expected to find herself wed to a man

*already married to the police department for the city
of New Orleans.*

DELLA AGREED TO JACK'S request and arranged to meet
him later that morning at the warehouse Eckton Computing had once leased. Perry had come along, leaving
Sugar Blues in Kachina's hands, and now sat with Jack
in his SUV, the heater running on high while they
waited for Book and Della.

The cold had settled in to stay, and Jack had left his
bomber jacket at her place. Watching him shiver in his
sweatshirt tugged at her heart. He'd obviously packed
light before leaving Texas, basing his needs on the un-
seasonable heat wave rather than the cold snap that had
blown in as predicted.

Then again, he'd probably grabbed what was closest
and hopefully clean. He didn't seem concerned with
much beyond simplicity. Except when it came to his
equipment. Both his laptop and his SUV were tricked
out with gadgets she'd never imagined existed.

To break the drive's uncomfortable silence, she'd
asked him about all she could see. He'd told her about
Becca, his assistant, and how his Yukon was his office
on wheels. But he hadn't been particularly chatty. And
soon she let him be, deciding he'd retreated into his
man cave and was feeling the need to brood.

Parked in front of the empty warehouse, one of
many in a long, unattended row, they soaked up the
heat in a silence broken only by the sports radio station
he'd tuned into. It was a distraction more than
anything, keeping them from having to talk. Keeping

him from having to admit she sat less than three feet away.

Obviously, she'd hit a hot button…or two or three or four…while ferreting out his scars. It didn't take a rocket scientist to figure out the damage inflicted hadn't all been to his body.

She hated this new tension that had sprung up between them. Tension was supposed to happen before sex, not afterward, making the air when they were together even harder to breathe. Sharing the front seat of his vehicle shouldn't be as unsettling as waiting for the results of medical tests.

And didn't that serve her right for thinking his invitation to sit in his lap was about more than sitting in his lap? Why she'd thought Jack would be different, that he'd finally be the one to think about sex with the head on his shoulders, still escaped her.

Men were all the same. They'd take their sports any way they could get them. On the field, the bed, the radio, grrr. She reached over, punched the buttons until she found a song that didn't make her think about drowning her sorrows in either a bottle of beer or the river.

She turned her head, stared out the window where the water of the Mississippi was as flat and gray as the sky above. And it wasn't until the one song had finished and the next began that she realized Jack was singing.

Straining to listen, she frowned, then closed her

eyes to focus. He didn't miss a beat. Not the lyrics. Not so much as a single note.

His voice was gruff, deep, a rock star's voice without the distortion of a mixer or a mike. It was a sexy sound, one that had her squirming in her seat, one that turned up the tension and the heat.

"You can sing," she finally said, glancing over.

"I can also play bass," he said, never looking her way.

"You didn't tell me."

He shrugged. "You didn't ask."

"I never had reason to." She waited, and when he said nothing more, she added, "Until now."

His mouth twitched, and he gave her a smile. "Does that mean you're asking?"

She couldn't believe the relief that came with that smile. "Yes. I'm asking."

"What exactly do you want to know?"

Why everything with you is a battle, for one thing. "When did you learn? How did you learn?"

"The bass I picked up listening to John Paul Jones, then I played it in band in high school."

She had no idea who John Paul Jones was and didn't care enough to ask. "What about the singing? Did you sing in school, too?"

He didn't say anything for so long that she didn't think he'd heard her, and she started to ask the question again. His shifting in his seat stopped her.

"No." He flexed the fingers he'd draped over the steering wheel. "I sang with a band for a while after getting out of the service."

The way he said it, "getting out", turned the expression into a statement. One that reminded her of Della's dismay at his suffering.

"A band I'd know?" she asked, when she didn't care about that either. What she wanted to know was what had gone on during his years of enlistment. If what Della had seen had happened then, or happened earlier.

"I doubt it. We played a lot of small clubs across the Southwest. Stayed on the west coast for several months."

"Did you record?"

He shook his head. "Nope. Just gave a lot of drunks music to pass out to."

Was that really what he thought? "You have a great voice. I'm sure you had fans."

"If we did, no one told me."

Or maybe you couldn't see them because that big chip on your shoulder was in the way. "Do you still play together? You never did tell me the name of the band."

"No. Our drummer took off on a trip with Mr. Ellis Dee and never came back." He reached down for the controls to his seat and moved all the way back, stretching his legs. "They called the band Diamond Jack."

"I'm sorry. For your friend."

He rolled his shoulders; she took it as a shrug of indifference. "We played together, traveled together. We weren't die-hard friends." And then he gave a soft chuckle.

"What?"

"What what?"

"You laughed."

"It's nothing. Just thinking about friends I had in high school. The ones I told you about last night. We played together in an ensemble. Now that was a band." He shook his head. "God, I miss those guys."

"A rock band? Like Diamond Jack."

"No. It wasn't that kind of band. It was about true blue school pride and winning competitions and trying to keep Heidi from killing Ben."

"Did she?" Perry asked, simply because she had no idea what else to say, and his trip down memory lane intrigued her.

"She did whack him upside the jaw one time with a bicycle chain."

"Ouch. What did he do to deserve that?"

"He offered to help her pay for college."

"And these are people you call friends?"

"They're the best." He laughed, laced his hands over his flat belly, closed his eyes and smiled. "They've been married now about six years, I guess."

She heard a tinge of envy in the affection with which he spoke. "Do you still see them?"

"When I can, sure. They live outside of Austin. My friend Quentin took all those blue ribbons we earned in competition and parlayed them into a nice career as a record producer. Randy's the only one of the bunch I haven't seen for a while."

Perry sighed. Hearing Jack talk about his friends made her realize how few she really had. At least, friends she would call close. She did have Claire as well as Chloe, Josie, Tally and Bree—all neighbors, and girlfriends she could count on for anything.

But she'd spent so much of her time for so many years running Sugar Blues for Della that she hadn't even developed those relationships as fully as she would have liked.

Maybe with the year so new, the time was right to change all of that. To step outside the safe little world she'd built for herself with her aunt, and experience more of life.

"What're you thinking about over there?"

She was not going to tell him…at least not right now. "Thinking that you were lucky in your friends."

"You didn't have any?"

"Not really." And how pitiful was that? "I think I scared everyone, first with my parents dying, then living with Della. I guess they thought I could read their minds or something. Whatever, they kept their distance."

"Well, you'll have to meet my bunch if you ever get to Austin."

She was saved having to digest what his offer meant by Book's car coming toward them. She pulled on her gloves and opened the door, letting in a whoosh of brisk air.

10

USING SUGAR'S gnarled walking stick, which Book retrieved from the attic after Perry's call, Della made her way from his car to the warehouse. The place had not been occupied since Eckton Computing had moved, yet appeared less unkempt than its neighbors.

Whether or not the condition of the property held any significance, she couldn't say. So far, she hadn't picked up but a flash or two of color. No heat. No sound. Nothing.

Facing the front of the structure, the cold wind whipping the ends of her scarf, she stared at the windows set high overhead that ran the length of the wall.

They looked out over the river, and she knew without going inside that a catwalk sat beneath. She also knew that Jack wouldn't find Dayton Eckhardt today.

He'd been here, though; she couldn't tell how recently, and since this building had once housed his firm's shipping, production and assembly departments, it wasn't exactly news that she sensed remnants of his energy.

She would need to get closer, to go inside…

"Is there any reason we can't go in?" she heard Jack ask of Book.

She glanced over, saw Book shrug. "As long as you don't bust out a window or take down a door, go ahead."

Della started toward the entrance on the far right, knowing when Jack reached it he'd find it unlocked. He did, turning the handle and pushing the door open, glancing in her direction with the air of a man holding an ace up his sleeve.

Della held back, not quite ready to enter, now that a sharp ice pick sensation had begun stabbing behind her right ear. "They've been here. They didn't see any reason to secure the place when they left."

"How long ago? Can you tell?" Book asked beside her as she slipped her hand into the crook of his elbow.

"I don't think but a few hours." She shook her head, narrowed her eyes. "I should be able to get a better sense once I'm inside."

"Do you think you should go in?" Perry asked, coming close to brush strands of hair, that had escaped the scarf, from Della's face. "You're so pale. Is it your foot?"

"No, my foot's fine. It's just…" Her shoes scraped over loose gravel as she hobbled closer to the door. "I haven't picked up spikes of anything for over forty-eight hours. I don't know what's different now unless—"

Black, everywhere black. A bolt of red, another of white. Lightning without thunder. Ripping through the sky. Water rushing madly.

A flood. Yellow rain. Drowning. Gasps of breath in bright orange. Rust and mud. The earth bubbling and swirling. Nowhere to hold on.

She groaned, stumbled back. Book caught her, and then Perry was there. "Della, sweetie? Can you hear me?"

It hurt to move her head. She tucked her forehead into Book's chest to hide from the knifelike pain. "Please. I need to go home. Take me home."

Cursing harshly beneath his breath, Book scooped her up in his arms and headed for the car. She kept her eyes closed, her head buried in the folds of his jacket.

His warmth soothed her, as did his scent, but she couldn't process any of what she'd seen. Not without the darkness of her room, her medication, and hours to sleep.

"I'll ride with you," Perry said, as Book settled Della into the front seat.

No. Her niece had to stay. That much she knew. Of that she was certain.

She reached out, grabbed Perry's wrist and squeezed. "No, Perry. You stay with Jack. He needs you."

"I'M SORRY. Really. That's the last thing I wanted to happen," Jack said, wondering if he could possibly feel worse.

Whatever he believed or didn't believe about Della Brazille's gift, he sure as hell would never have asked her to come here if he'd thought it would make her sick.

"I don't think she expected it." Perry rubbed at her

wrist, a frown on her face as she watched Book drive away. The detective hadn't looked too happy with Jack—or with Perry, either.

After getting Della situated, Book had given his business card to Jack and taken him aside, ordering him to call if he found anything, and not to touch whatever he did.

Jack wasn't stupid. He was, in fact, as much a professional as the other man. But he'd let the detective have his say and had kept his resentment to a simmer.

Figuring out the reason for Book's barely veiled threat hadn't required a PhD. Had Jack been in the other man's shoes, he wasn't sure he wouldn't have punctuated his directive with a fist.

Then again, that was something he'd never know, seeing how his woman wasn't the one hurting. He turned to Perry. She looked strange. Strained.

And he had to remind himself that she wasn't his woman. "You could have gone with them. You didn't have to stay."

"Yes, I did," was all she said before facing him, her cheeks apple red from the wind. "So? What are you waiting for?"

Nothing, he supposed. Except something about Della's reaction had him wondering if he shouldn't do this solo while Perry waited outside. If anything happened to her…

Cursing under his breath, he pulled a flashlight from his pocket and switched it on, making sure the one he'd given Perry worked as well. "You can wait in the truck if you want to. You don't have to come with me."

"Actually, I do." She swiped at her hair with gloved hands. "I'm under strict orders."

To do what? Babysit? "Orders from who?"

"Della."

He let that sink in, and decided he didn't like it. He didn't like it at all. Still, whatever she'd seen, she obviously wouldn't have told Perry to stay if doing so would put her in danger.

"Okay, then. Let's do it," he said, and pushed through the door.

Perry followed. "I'm surprised Book didn't want you to wait until he could get back."

With Della ordering Perry to stay, Jack doubted Book would be budging from Della's side until this crisis had passed. "I'm pretty sure he thinks this is a wild-goose chase."

"Even with what Della has seen?"

"She hasn't pinpointed a location. Hell, she hasn't even seen any chickens. Her visions could be of Timbuktu, for all we know."

They certainly weren't of this place—not if they were flashes of colors and light like Perry had described. The warehouse was nothing but a cold, bleak cavern. Concrete floors and cinderblock walls in matching shades of gray.

Dust motes danced in the trace of dead light drifting down from the dirty windows. A staircase on the right rose to a catwalk built against all four walls, and a row of upstairs offices at the rear of the structure.

"I can see why Book didn't stick around," Perry said from Jack's side.

But Jack hadn't been interested in the detective. His own research had told him the warehouse was empty. What he'd wanted to find out was whether or not there was anything here that *couldn't* be seen.

Since he was already tottering on a very shaky limb, he was going to take Della's reaction to mean that there was. His only hope was that a search of the place might turn up a clue he could follow, or a hint of where to go from here.

"Is this where Taylor's husband worked?" Perry asked, walking toward the center of the room.

Jack nodded, listening to the echo of her steps and her voice. "I don't know how many shifts they worked here then, but he was lead boss for one of the production crews."

"What does that mean?"

"You got me."

She crossed her arms, rubbed them from her elbows to her shoulders. When she exhaled, her breath frosted. And Jack grew even colder.

"So what's the plan?" she asked. "You want me to see what's upstairs while you check out the first floor?"

He hadn't thought much beyond getting inside. "It might be best if we stay together."

"It might be faster, and warmer, if we don't."

It wasn't that he didn't trust her…

"Unless you don't trust me?" she asked, backing toward the staircase with a dare in her eyes.

The risers looked sturdy enough—though her expression left him unbalanced—and he nodded, listening to the metallic ringing of her footsteps echo as she climbed.

Since there was nothing at the front of the bottom floor, the place having obviously been gutted and still waiting for a new tenant, he headed for the rear, where he found two empty restrooms.

The doors were ajar, the toilet tanks long empty, the water pipes clamped tight to the bottoms of the sinks and the walls. He shone his flashlight overhead in both rooms, and found identical bare bulbs with pull strings. The floor drains were dry and as clean as they got in a place like this.

He found no fresh graffiti, and no meaning in what he could read of that which was there. No wastebaskets, no toilet paper, air dryers that were empty of everything but air when he pried them from the walls.

He made a cursory trip around the cavernous room, flicking his light up and down the walls from the floor to the catwalk above. Nothing. Anything Della had sensed had made no lasting mark here.

Just as he started for the stairs, Perry called his name. He glanced overhead, saw her at the catwalk railing waving him up. He took the stairs two at a time, his feet pounding against the metal.

Something in her face told him to hurry. Something in his gut told him to run.

"What?" he asked, before he'd even reached the top. "What did you find?"

She shook her head, her eyes wide and glassy, her face a deathly pale. "It's not good."

He reached for her, wrapped his hand around her shoulder and squeezed. "Are you okay?"

"I will be," she said, her voice as faint as her nod.

She took a step in reverse, then turned and made her way down the catwalk. His heart was pounding from both dread and adrenaline as he followed her to the third door in the long row of five.

He stepped through, shone his flashlight around the small office space. Unlike the floor below, this room hadn't been emptied. Industrial gray file cabinets lined one wall, a matching desk backed up to another, but he saw nothing in the low-ceilinged space to explain Perry's alarm.

"At the end of the row of file cabinets," she said from his shoulder. "There's a door. Into a closet."

And that was when his own panic set in. He inhaled, exhaled, inhaled, exhaled, the short choppy breaths frosting in cloudbursts of white.

He reminded himself of where he was—New Orleans; of who he was with—Perry Brazille; of the reason he was here—Dayton Eckhardt—before he walked to the corner. He saw the spray-painted message first.

There will be no ransom demand. We have what we want.

And then he saw the chair, the ropes hanging from the legs and the arms. Yellow nylon, a water-skier's ropes. Ropes used to bind cargo, to secure it on the deck of a ship.

To secure a man below in the hold, leaving him in the dark for days. For weeks. Until he lost count. Until he barely remembered his name.

"I'm guessing that's his finger?"

At Perry's question, Jack startled. The flashlight beam danced around the small room as he forced his breathing pattern to return to normal, forced his muscles to relax, hoping doing so would calm the near deadly beat of his heart.

What had she asked him? "Finger?"

"On the floor," she said, and he looked down to where she pointed.

Yeah. It was a finger. He ground his jaw until he felt a joint pop, then he stepped into the small room, checking behind the door, shining his light into the corners.

It took only seconds to see what he needed to see. He stepped back out. "Did you touch anything in here?"

"I pushed the door open." She held up both hands. "But I'm wearing gloves."

He nodded, guided her back to the staircase with one hand on her arm. Once at the top of the stairs, he pocketed his flashlight, dug for Book's card and pulled his cell from his waistband holster.

"It's Jack. You need to get a crime scene unit to the warehouse as soon as you can."

JACK SAT on the running board of his SUV, the door open, the engine running, the heater blowing at full blast. He had his arms crossed, his hands tucked in his armpits, the hood of his sweatshirt pulled almost to his mouth.

Perry had bummed a Styrofoam cup from one of the

officers on the scene, and then bummed coffee from the thermos of another. She held it beneath his nose and waited.

It didn't take long for him to look up and push back the hood. He took the cup from her gloved hand with a muttered "Thanks," as he wrapped all ten of his fingers around it.

"You're welcome. And you look like shit." She hadn't planned to blurt it out like that, but he did. If possible, he looked as if he'd aged ten years in the last ten minutes.

He sipped, grimaced. "Thanks for that, too."

"Seriously, Jack. It's more than a lack of sleep." She'd hazard a guess that it was more than this case. "You look like a ghost. Or at least like you've seen one."

"Nah. Just a finger," he said, and sipped again.

Jack Montgomery, Private Eye, reduced to a shell of his former self by a severed finger? She wasn't buying it.

But before she could say anything else, he asked, "They found the ring, right? Behind the door?"

She leaned against the vehicle's closed back passenger door. "Believe it or not, yes."

"They bagged the ropes? And took scrapings from the spray paint?"

"And confiscated the chair."

"Did they spray it with luminol or fluorescein?"

"I don't know," she said, and turned, leaning her shoulder against the frame and staring down at the top of his head.

"Okay. Whatever."

"You know, Jack. I'm a shop clerk. They're not exactly giving me a blow-by-blow. I heard about the ring, the rope and the chair while I was hunting down coffee. If you want to know more, you're going to have to put those investigative skills of yours to work."

He studied the coffee in his cup for so long that she wondered if he'd been listening, or if he'd returned to wherever the scene upstairs had taken him. He'd said little about what they'd discovered. She'd expected so much more.

She'd expected him to be ecstatic, to be juiced on adrenaline to the point where he wasn't even feeling the cold. Instead, he sat hunched over, alone, as if he weren't the victor but the victim.

The same victim Della had witnessed suffering when she'd done nothing more that morning in her kitchen than reach over and touch his arm.

"Jack? Are you okay?"

"I need to talk to Della. I need to know exactly what she saw. If it makes any sense in context."

"If she saw chickens, you mean."

He tossed back the rest of the coffee, threw the cup over his shoulder into the SUV's back floorboard, and got to his feet. "Did Book say anything about how she was feeling?"

"No, but I can tell you she'll be sleeping until the headache subsides," Perry said, glancing up at the sound of footsteps approaching.

Book reached them and stopped, gripping the top

of Jack's open door, his expression grim. "Well, it's an official case now. Which means, we'll take it from here. I need you to come with me to operations. Fill me in on what happened and what else you know."

Jack grumbled under his breath, but said, "Sure. Just let me drop Perry off with Della first."

"I need to get statements from both of you," Book argued, one hand moving to his waist. "Kachina said she'd check in on Della until one of us gets back."

"How was she when you left?" Perry asked.

"Sleeping. She went out fast."

"Good. We'll go and get this done while she's asleep," Perry said, circling the front of the vehicle on her way to the passenger side.

"Right behind you," Book said to Jack before jogging back to the taped-off scene, and his own car parked just outside.

"Are you going to tell him what you know?" she asked, once Jack was settled behind the wheel.

"I don't have any reason not to. But anything he gets from me, he could get from the Austin police."

He shifted into drive and headed out. She waited until they'd turned and left the warehouse behind before asking, "What are you going to do now?"

"Once we're done at the station, talk to Della, find out what she can tell me about what she saw. Assuming what she sees is even real."

Perry knew he wasn't going to like it, but tossed out the challenge anyway. "There's one way to find out, you know."

He cast her a wary glance. "What's that?"

"Test her gift for yourself."

"And how do I do that?"

"Have her do a reading."

11

AFTER PERRY CHECKED in on Della, Jack gave in to the insistence of both women that he schedule the reading for midnight. Della was confident she'd be feeling better by then, and Perry didn't want to wait because, well, he wasn't sure why except that she was intent on proving a point.

He wasn't thrilled with the idea. Neither was he thrilled to admit that Perry *did* have a point, but there really wasn't any way around it.

If Della could pick up enough vibes in his aura, or fluctuations in the cosmos, or woo-woo type echo things to see the truth of his past, then maybe he could get this case rolling again. And maybe, just maybe, he wouldn't feel like such a putz for partnering up with a psychic.

Because that's exactly what he felt like. A putz.

His investigator's nose had brought him to New Orleans to look into Eckhardt's roots, and his instinct for survival had led him to Café Eros.

His belief that he'd spotted a scam had taken him to Sugar Blues, his certainty that all trails went somewhere to the *Times-Picayune*.

Refusing to believe in coincidences had sent him to Eckton Computing's warehouse, which had turned out to be the end of his line.

He'd been able to run the investigation on his own as long as the official case was still in Texas. But now that it had crossed state lines, he had nothing left to go on but instinct.

Instinct, and a psychic. And if that didn't define a putz, he didn't know what did.

Leaving Perry at Sugar Blues once they'd finished giving Detective Franklin their statements, Jack put in another call to update Cindy Eckhardt, then spent the rest of the day tracking down friends of Bob and Dawn Taylor, as well as Eckton employees who had worked with Taylor.

What Jack found out was that the co-workers weren't surprised Taylor hadn't found work after the Eckton layoffs. His reputation as a hard-assed, hard-headed, hard-drinking bastard had made the industry rounds.

What had bowled them over was his suicide. No one thought a man that mean had it in him to take himself out. Nor did Jack get the sense that any of them mourned the man's passing.

If Taylor were still alive, several had said they could see him scheming to get back at Eckhardt, but since he wasn't around to sever fingers they really couldn't help.

The couple's personal friends Jack had managed to catch up with repeated what he'd already learned. Everyone was sorry for Dawn. The men were anxious to do anything they could to her, uh, for her. The women knew that, and felt she would do better if they all gave her time to grieve. Twelve months' worth of time.

Right. With friends like that…

By the time Jack returned to Sugar Blues, it was close to ten. He had no idea if the women had eaten, so he brought a bag of burgers and fries for three just in case.

He parked in the alley behind the shop and knocked when he reached the new back door. He saw Perry through the window over the sink, and seconds later she pushed the curtain aside to see who was there.

She was smiling when she opened the door. "You ought to give me your cell phone number. I just realized that I don't have a way to get in touch with you."

"You thought I'd skip town before you got the results of my reading?" he asked, setting the food on the table and thinking that he kinda liked the idea of being nagged if Perry was the one doing the nagging. She was sweet. She was cute. He could get used to having her around.

"Of course not," she said as she closed the door. "Whatever happens tonight is between you and Della." And then she sighed. "Mmm. Onions and mustard and grease. It smells wonderful."

He gestured toward the seat next to his. "Pull up a chair. I brought plenty."

"Ooh, thanks." She beat him to tearing open the bag. "Della's still sleeping, and Kachina had appointments until eight. I just finished closing up and I'm starving."

He unfolded the waxed paper around his burger and dumped out his fries, then reached for a squeeze packet of ketchup. "I'm surprised you have enough business to work the hours you do. And that it's enough for the two of you to live on."

"Three," she said, dragging a fry through his ketchup and shoving it into her mouth.

"Three?" he echoed, because there was something about a woman with an appetite that made him forget his worries.

"Kachina makes three."

"Hmm. I'm not sure I can afford your services."

She sputtered. "For you, cher? No charge."

His cares went the way of his worries with the Cajun flavor she added to her offer. This was the first time all day he'd been able to relax, and damn if it didn't feel great. "Thanks. I think."

"What, you need client testimonials?"

"To prove I'm getting my money's worth?" He took a bite of his burger, sat back and chewed.

"I was thinking more along the lines of proving that you're not wasting your time." She picked up another fry, attacked his ketchup again.

He frowned. "I'm here, aren't I?"

"Only because it's too late to bother any more of the Big Easy's fine citizens. And," she added, wrapping both hands around her hamburger bun, "because Book warned you to keep your nose out of his business."

Yeah, it was his business all right. "He wouldn't have half of what he does if I hadn't given it to him."

"And that just grates, doesn't it?" she asked, a tad too smugly.

He reached over while her hands were full and filched a half dozen of her fries. "Only because Detective Franklin's working with some sort of chip on his shoulder."

"Oh, what? And you're not?"

"Not really," he said, and chomped down.

"Jack Montgomery." She turned in her chair to face him. "Do I need to get you a mirror?"

Chewing, he glanced over, surprised by her incredulous tone.

He had baggage; who didn't? But to call it a chip? Did he really heave his past around as if it might fall and crush anyone he allowed to get close?

He shrugged. "Maybe I am. It's not such a big deal."

"If you say so," she said, and went back to eating. "Though you might want to make sure it doesn't get so heavy that you end up getting hurt."

He wondered what she knew about hurt. Then he remembered the death of her parents and wanted to kick his own insensitive ass.

Still, insensitive or not, he was curious. And so he asked, "Is that what happened to you? You carried a chip for too long?"

She gave a sharp, unladylike snort. "You mean why did I decide to sleep with you after six years of sleeping with no one?"

Well, there was that. He had to admit he was curious. "Sure. We can start there."

"Okay, fine." She reached for a napkin, wiped her

mouth and hands, then got up to get two sodas from the fridge. "Because of that chemistry thing. And because I like you. A lot. A whole lot," she added softly, as if speaking to herself. "I like your honesty. Your integrity. You're sexy as hell. Then there's the fact that you're good around the house."

"Next, you'll be saying I've got a super personality," he said, though he couldn't help but get a nice buzz from her comments.

She handed him his can and popped the top on hers before she sat back down. "I've spent most of my life in the company of women. And all of my formative years when I learned the differences a Y chromosome can make."

Him? He liked the differences, and started to say so.

But she quickly cut him off, waving one hand, her other wrapped around her soda. "And I don't just mean the differences in the equipment. I mean the differences in what using the equipment means."

Oh. That. "So, that was the reason for your trip into the closet this morning?"

"No. I was just waiting for you to make coffee."

"Right."

She rolled her eyes. "Yes. I was angry."

"With me?"

"With both of us."

"The crack about conserving water—"

"Wasn't any worse than mine about rings." She breathed deeply, then took a drink. "I was frustrated. And, yes. I was hurt. I wasn't sure what to expect from you the morning after. And I didn't understand the one-night-stand vibes you gave off."

He was an ass. Seriously. An ass in over his head with this particular gypsy woman. To be honest, she'd scared him shitless. "I'm sorry. I didn't—"

"But you did. We spent an amazing night and an amazing morning, and the first thing you say to me is that it was only sex." She sighed, shrugged, sipped. "And maybe it was for you. But I let my emotions get in the way, and ended up with a big 'what the hell am I doing?' moment."

"Because you leapt without looking."

"Exactly. And I don't leap. Not anymore."

"What happened six years ago?" he found himself asking, when it shouldn't matter and it wasn't any of his business.

"I came to work for Della full-time and stopped playing at getting a degree."

"Who was it? A fellow student or a professor?"

She stuck out her tongue. "A TA, if you must know. He was in it for the fun and games. And I wanted something more. See? The two just don't mix."

"I can't imagine you writing off relationships based on one bad deal," he said, almost choking at the "r" word he let slip. Was that where they were headed?

"And what do you mean, you can't imagine me doing that? We had a one-night stand. I don't see how that qualifies you as a Perry expert."

He shook his head as he pushed away from the table.

She sat back—arms crossed, chin lifted—and he

knew the battle was on. "Fine. Then explain to me why you think you know what you know."

The woman was driving him mad. "You, Ms. Brazille, are an open book."

Her lips pruned up. "You don't say."

"I do say. Anyone who spends any length of time with you can tell what you're thinking."

"Oh, really?" she said, tapping one foot. "And what am I thinking now, Jack, huh? What am I thinking now?"

She was thinking he'd hit too close to a truth she didn't want to admit, and she didn't like it at all. She didn't like being as easy to read as she was. She didn't like that she'd allowed herself to be hurt—or that he was the one who'd done it.

She believed in astrological animals and ghosts that sang in stairwells and whatever the hell rune stones were, but she couldn't bring herself to believe that he'd figured her out in only a matter of days. Neither did she seem to be buying that he'd never intended her harm.

And he'd about had it with that. He reached for the leg of her chair and hauled hers up against his. Then he planted his hands on either side of her hips, holding on to the seat as he held on to her gaze.

Once he knew he had her attention, once he saw the flutter of her pulse in her throat, he leaned closer, bringing his mouth inches from hers before saying, "I don't know about you, but this is the only thing I'm thinking."

And then he moved in for the kiss. She was warm

and willing. She smelled like the spices he knew, tasted like salt and ketchup and the same dinner they'd both eaten. The thought made him chuckle.

His laughter made her groan. "I know. Onions."

"They've never tasted better," he assured her, and went back for more. She brought her arms around his neck, and somehow ended up in his lap in his chair.

It was exactly where he wanted her, exactly where he needed her to be. She caught at his lower lip, pulling him into her mouth, bathing him with her tongue, nipping him with her teeth.

He liked the way she nipped, that she wasn't afraid she might hurt him, that she let him nip her back and laughed when he did.

It was the perfect battle of wills, the perfect parry and thrust. Their tongues mating, teasing, playing. He didn't think he would ever get enough.

He slipped his hand to her back, eased his fingers beneath the hem of her sweater, kneaded circles up her spine until he found the clasp of her bra. He freed it, and she gasped into his mouth. A gasp followed quickly by a giggle.

He didn't think he'd ever met another woman who laughed at such inopportune times, and he loved every single sound that spilled from her throat. He also loved the way she twisted and turned until his hand covered her breast.

He thought back to the way she'd looked in the shower, how pale her skin, how dark her nipples, and he found her areola and stroked the puckered skin.

She moaned and squirmed, and he pinched her

nipple, kneaded her breast, shoved his tongue into her mouth and made sure she knew he was thinking about shoving it into a certain part of her body that tasted salty and warm and marine.

And then he was the one groaning, the one on the edge of coming apart. And he was the one wanting her mouth sucking on more than his tongue, licking at more than his lips.

Give him five seconds, ten seconds max, that's all he needed and he could have her on the edge of the table, her skirt up to her waist, his fly open, her thighs wrapped around his hips…

A softly cleared throat brought him careening to a mental *coitus interruptus*. Perry unwound her arms from his neck and pushed back with her hands on his chest.

He did his best to slip his hand from beneath her sweater without drawing Della's notice. But when Perry started to push out of his lap, he held her there, hiding the bulging proof of their indiscretion beneath her skirt.

"Don't mind me," Della said, thumping with her walking stick into the room. "I only came for a bottle of water." She crossed to the fridge for her drink, then returned the way she came. "I'll be in the reading room when you're ready, Jack."

Once the thump of the walking stick faded, Perry asked, "Are you ready?"

No, the reminder of what lay ahead had pretty much taken all the ready right out of him. "Shouldn't you be asking me if I have any last wishes? Or what I want for my final meal?"

"I thought that's what I just did," she teased, climbing from his lap and waiting for him to gather up his balls and get on with it.

THE ROOM DELLA USED for her readings was small, no larger than the bathroom off the kitchen. He didn't have a blueprint to go by, but Jack was pretty sure the two shared a communal wall.

The entrance was marked by a curtain of blue beads, a twin to the one that led from the shop into the kitchen hallway. This one he'd never seen before, tucked as it was into the far corner of Sugar Blues.

The room was lit by a single-bulb lamp that hung low on a chain from the ceiling. In the center of the room was a table. Beneath the table, two chairs. On top, a dark bowl of water-covered petals.

The petals were fresh. He could smell the floral aroma as soon as he entered the room. He waited for Della to speak. She said nothing, did no more than indicate he should sit in the closest chair.

She took the other, facing him and asking him to place his hands, palms down, on either side of the bowl. Her voice, when she made the request, was barely audible. Her eyes, which hadn't yet made contact with his, appeared hazy and lost. He supposed it was more like a trance than confusion.

The chair was comfortable enough, the seat and back both covered in a dark blue velvet, and the smell of the flower petals was soothing, like lavender or jasmine.

He figured the water could have turned them blue

since he didn't think either of them were. But then he quit thinking of anything because Della dipped her fingertips into the water before she placed them over his.

Her skin was cool, as was the water, her touch calming and light. He wasn't sure where to look, and so he focused on her face. Her eyes were clear as she stared into the bowl.

"You've been hurt," she finally said, her voice soft, the words even. "You've also hurt others."

None of that was news, or specific enough to cause a blip in his pulse. He figured, in fact, that it was a fairly universal complaint.

"Choosing the military over moving with your family was the best choice. You need to stop wondering and move on."

Thinking about Janie, about his parents, about how he'd failed them emotionally by not being there… His chest tightened, the fingers of his left hand twitched and he would have made a fist had Della not been holding him in place. Funny, she didn't seem that strong.

And, really. It wouldn't have been hard to discover the reasons for the choice he'd made. His friends in Austin knew, though he couldn't quite see Della calling up any of them to ask.

She inhaled deeply, exhaled slowly. The tips of her fingers flexed; her touch stroked over his knuckles. "Having met you, I can't say I'm surprised you drew the attention of your superiors so quickly. You're not an easy man to overlook."

He hadn't thought to ask in advance if he was allowed to talk. And so he said nothing instead of telling her that what got him noticed was the same thing that got him into trouble. Trying to make a difference.

He didn't do well with authority. Not when those in such positions wouldn't give him the one thing, the only thing, he wanted. Logical reasons for the decisions they made. "That's the way it's always been done," just didn't cut it. That mindset stopped progress in its tracks, kept good men from making a difference.

"That path isn't always the easiest one to take." Della's fingers slid over his knuckles and the backs of his hands before growing still. "And the price can be so very great."

But military men and women paid it on a daily basis, and not just in ongoing wars in places like Afghanistan and Iraq. Also in covert operations infiltrating terrorist cells around the world, to gather information to bring them down, and thwart future attacks being planned.

"Most leave their tours never experiencing a gunshot. But you carry scars from several." Her fingers searched out the pressure points between his bones, pressing lightly, sliding to his wrists then back. "You've seen more conflict than a man should ever see."

He wasn't about to argue with that.

"But there is one incident that won't let you go."

He hadn't even swallowed and still he nearly choked, waiting, waiting…his blood pounding its way through his veins. God, he hoped she wasn't going to say what he feared. He didn't want her to know. He didn't want anyone to know. He didn't want to remember. He didn't want to forget.

Dark eyes against skin that should not have been so deathly pale. Shackles securing the unwitting prisoners. Chains thicker than the human limbs they bound. Mewling, desperate noises.

"The men you freed don't go a day without thanking you. They offer up prayers for your health and longevity."

And still he waited, only this time he did so with his gut so painfully knotted he had to fight the urge to double over and crawl beneath the table.

"They wonder how long you were kept without being allowed to eat. Or to drink. They spill their own blood, hoping your God will replace what you lost with their offering."

It had begun with his pride and his dignity, and had swiftly spiraled down until he came close to losing his mind. He'd lost enough that he'd no longer known night from day, minutes from hours from weeks. He'd lost enough that he'd no longer known if the faces he saw were real or monsters in his dreams…

He'd lost enough that he'd given up on living.

"They go to their wives at night and sleep close to the soft, precious bodies they never thought they'd see again. They don't shut their eyes until they picture you at peace and at rest and in love."

Those men, those men. He could see every minute of the torture they'd endured. Except he couldn't see anything at all because his eyes were filled with the tears flowing down his cheeks.

A sob caught in his chest. He fought to hold it back. It escaped in the same heated, panicked rush as the men he'd released from their cage.

He heard the splash of water as they dived overboard, swimming for the life raft he'd cut loose hours before. He'd always wondered if they'd made it, if they'd lived, if they'd died.

He'd never wondered if they thought about him. He'd never thought himself worth it. He'd been a part of the group that had rounded them up and stolen them from their village, from their families. He didn't deserve their prayers or their thanks.

If anything, he had deserved to die.

12

PERRY HAD spent the last half hour alone, pacing the kitchen, instead of heading upstairs to bed. She had a thousand questions she wanted to ask of both Jack and Della, but she knew that she never would.

She wanted to go home. She wanted Jack to go with her. Yet she wasn't comfortable leaving Della alone.

All her indecisiveness meant was that she did nothing constructive during the wait except put clean sheets on the bed in the utility room, just in case Jack stayed.

Because, honestly? She had no idea what he was going to do after tonight. He'd run all the leads he'd mentioned, and that was before Book had made it clear that it was now Jack's job to butt out.

She didn't see that happening, but she was clueless as to what he was going to do. If he had any plans, he hadn't shared them. And being kept in the dark was driving her insane.

But the real crazy maker of the moment was wanting to know what was going on in the reading room. And that she would never find out unless Jack decided to tell her. That was another thing she didn't see happening.

In fact, she couldn't help wondering if Della was getting any reaction from him at all. If the reading didn't go well, if Jack came out of the experience still doubting Della's gift, and had nowhere else to turn…

At the sound of the beaded curtain stirring, Perry turned and looked up from the refrigerator—into which she'd been blindly staring—in time to see Jack barge into the kitchen, and slam straight out the back door.

Frowning, she closed the fridge, thinking it was a good thing the new door was sturdier than the old, what with the way it bounced off the wall with a thud loud enough to wake the dead. She crossed the room to close it, but was stopped halfway there by her aunt.

"Don't shut him out," Della said, standing in the kitchen entrance, her face drawn, her eyes damp. "Go to him. He needs you."

The words were an echo of what she'd said this morning. Perry started to ask what had happened, but closed her mouth at the shake of Della's head and the walking stick she lifted to point the way.

Perry's nerves shivered like flowers in the rain. She flipped the light switch, plunging the kitchen into darkness, and opened the door.

The moon was high and bright, the streetlamps on either end of the alley shining down. It was enough light for her to see where she was going, and to see where Jack was pacing a circle around the empty fountain.

She cut in behind him on his next trip around, and boosted herself up to sit on the concrete ledge. She didn't want to say anything to set him off or to hurt him, so she grabbed the first innocuous thought that came to mind.

"This is exactly where Della was sitting when Book first met her. It was as cold then as it is now, but that night the fountain was on, and she was soaked by the time I made it here from Court du Chaud."

Jack didn't say anything, but his steps did slow. Perry wasn't sure that was such a good thing since the aerobic exercise was the only thing keeping him warm. That, and the fury or rage or whatever was clearly burning him up.

She had no way of knowing, so she continued to talk. "There had been a break-in next door. It went down pretty badly, someone ended up getting killed. Book and his partner were the ones who responded."

Jack had quit circling the fountain and was now pacing back and forth in front of her. He'd stuffed his hands deep into his pockets and hunched his shoulders for warmth.

She wanted to go to him, to wrap him in her arms, to take away whatever it was he was feeling. She wanted to know what had happened during the reading, but could only hear her aunt's words insisting that he needed her here.

"It's amazing she didn't catch pneumonia. She was wearing pajamas, and not very warm ones at that. We finally got her inside, and Book stayed to take her statement."

Perry's teeth began to chatter, and she crossed her arms and huddled in on herself. "I've lost track of how many times she's helped him since. And I keep wondering if they're going to get together. They make such a great couple, though I'm pretty sure neither one…"

She let the thought trail because Jack had stopped. He stood on the sidewalk facing her, his hands still in his pockets, his shoulders still stooped.

But the moon was shining down just so, and she could see lines of pain etched on his face, the tracks of tears she doubted he knew he'd cried streaking his cheeks.

"Oh, Jack," she said, her chest tightening until she thought she wouldn't be able to breathe. "What happened to you?"

It was all she got out, and his only answer was to look away, jerk his hands from his pockets and scrub them over his face, shaking his head as he did.

The sound he made then was a mad howl of anger, a gut-ripping wail that tore her heart. She didn't know what to do, didn't know what to say. She caught back a sob and waited, because that was when he turned.

He turned, and he came toward her, and before she could do more than blink he was holding her head to keep her from moving while he covered her mouth with his.

He stepped between her legs when she spread them, cradled her face, slid his tongue between her lips and devoured her. She brought her hands up to his shoulders, clawing at the fabric of his shirt to hold on.

He was shaking when he moved his hands to her thighs and started rucking up her skirt until her legs were bare and he could get to her panties.

When he hooked a finger over the fabric of the crotch, she gasped into his mouth. When he found her wet and ready, he growled and pushed a finger inside. She gripped his shoulders to keep from falling back and further widened her legs.

And then his hands were at his fly and he was lifting himself out of his boxers and jeans. She held on to the ledge at her hips, bracing her weight there and hooking her heels behind him.

He moved in, tore her panties out of the way and positioned himself at her entrance. And then, his gaze locked furiously with hers, he pushed in.

It was an agonizingly slow penetration. He took his time stretching her open when what she wanted was to be filled with him now. But she let him take her, possess her, surround himself with her as it seemed he needed to do.

And then he began to move, and she scooted her hips forward, knowing this wasn't about any emotion beyond what she'd seen in his face and heard in his voice.

It was about survival and being alive and being human and being good enough. It was a validation, and that was all she needed to know. She gave him all that she could of her body.

And when he came, when he tossed back his head and cried out his release, when he returned to her, wrapped her in his arms and held her until she felt she would break, that's when she gave him her love.

THEY LAY together afterwards in the utility room's twin bed. It was a tight fit, but neither minded. They'd shed all of their clothes, and the nearness allowed them to experience the pleasures of intimacy with nothing in the way.

It was what Perry had been wanting forever. And the idea that she'd known Jack less than four days didn't even make sense. What made sense was this. Being here with him. Skin to skin. Touching him and never saying a word.

She couldn't even talk about what had happened outside. Words failed her, as did understanding. The loss of her parents had been a horrific event, but it was one she had learned to live with.

Whether or not he believed in ghosts, Jack was haunted. And she knew this wasn't about his family. What he fought against, what he fended off, what he hid from, she didn't know. She might never know. She only knew that was his truth.

All she could do was be what he needed. He was here and he was with her. For now, maybe for longer, that was enough.

She rolled toward him, her breasts flattened against his chest, her knee flung over his. He lay with his elbow beneath his head, and used the fingers of his other hand to play between her legs.

She pulled in a sharp breath, wishing the room wasn't so dark, wanting to see his eyes. She supposed he didn't want anything of the sort, not after the breakdown she'd witnessed outside.

His index finger was long and thick, and she loved how he used his hands, loved the way he teased her, stroking and circling and dipping in and out until she was panting and so very close to coming undone.

Shuddering, she kissed his chest, scrunching up her nose when his hair tickled. She found his nipple, swirled her tongue around the flat disc, used her fingertips to massage the muscle there.

He groaned, and his erection prodded her belly, bobbing against her as if knocking to come in. Smiling to herself, she pushed him onto his back and climbed over him, straddling his hips, her hands on his shoulders, her breasts swinging above his mouth.

He pressed them together, sucked at one nipple then at the other until moisture began to trickle down her thighs. She reached down and wrapped her hand around his shaft, rubbing the head of his cock through her folds.

He moved his hands to her hips, guiding her as she took him inside. She lowered herself slowly, leaning back and bracing her palms just above his knees for the ride.

It was a sweet grinding pressure, the up and down motion, the fullness of his erection spreading her wide. She pushed up on her knees. He followed, lifting his hips off the bed.

They came down together, and then he held her still, sliding his hands up her thighs, capturing her clit between his thumbs.

She strained against the sensations that seized her. She wasn't ready. She wanted to wait. She hadn't yet had enough of him, his mouth, his fingers, his cock.

And so she leaned over him, her palms flat on the bed above his shoulders, and took what she wanted from his mouth. She kissed him with a fierceness that surprised her. She hadn't known how deeply her hunger ran, how very deeply her love did.

His return kiss matched her fever, his tongue sliding over hers, his lips bruising. He lifted one knee and bumped her sideways. She fell to the mattress; still buried inside her body, he followed her over.

And then he was above her, looming, hovering, groaning when he couldn't wait anymore. He hooked her knees over his forearms and drove forward, again and again.

Since there wasn't a headboard to keep her there, the pounding nearly drove her off the bed. The springs creaked and the frame shook until she finally planted her palms overhead to keep from bouncing against the wall.

And then she closed her eyes and rode out the storm, letting Jack take her where he wanted to go. He dropped his head to his chest, his eyes screwed tightly shut, his arms straining to bear the weight of his motion, his hips shaking as he came.

She followed him seconds later, the vibrating pressure between her legs the push that sent her over. She cried out, slapped her hands against the mattress, flexed her fingers into the sheet on either side of her hips and held on.

He ground down against her, and she straightened her legs, pushing her clit up against the base of his shaft. It was almost too much, the sharp bursts of pleasure bordering on pain, and she whimpered as he rolled them both to their sides.

"You okay?" he whispered, and she nodded.

"A bit too much of a good thing, is all," she said, feeling the burn of raw skin.

He reached up, brushed her hair from her eyes. "You should've said something."

"No. It was a good thing, remember?" She rubbed her face against his palm and purred.

"Yeah, well, let me...do this." He eased his body from hers, then reached for the blanket they'd kicked to the end of the bed and pulled it over them both. "There. That's better, yes?"

"Yes, much," she said, nodding rapidly as if the movement would keep unexpected tears from spilling. After-sex hormonal overload, that was all it was. Tight-wire emotions finally set free.

"Perry?"

She sniffed. "Jack?"

"You're not crying, are you?"

"Not really." This was so embarrassing. "Just sort of...leaking."

"If I scared you outside earlier, or hurt you—"

"No, it's not that. Not really." She wasn't even sure she could explain it to herself.

And then she felt him tense. "If you don't want to be here—"

"Oh, no. Don't even think that for a minute." She found his hand, cradled it between both of hers, lacing all of their fingers together. "There's no place I want to be more."

"Including your own bed?"

"Right now? No. It's too big."

"And this one's not too small?"

"Size isn't everything, you know."

"Hmm. And here I'd been under the impression that it was the only thing that mattered."

She sighed, loving how easy he was to be with, to tease with. "I suppose in some cases it does matter."

"Such as?"

"Like when buying in bulk."

He snorted. "Does anyone really need that much of anything? Think about it. You buy it, don't use it, it goes bad. Then you're out a lot of money on all those ruined condoms."

She laughed. She couldn't help it. "So, less is more, then?"

"Less is at least worth considering," he said.

"Sorta like quality versus quantity?"

He pulled his hand from hers, draped it over her hip and pulled her close, caressing her back and her bottom and the length of her thigh. She closed her eyes and tucked both of her hands beneath her cheek as if in prayer.

Because, in a way, that's exactly what she was doing. Praying that he wasn't going to walk out of her life. She knew so very little about him. She wasn't ready to let him go.

"I'm not sure how much longer I'll be here. It's going to depend on where the case takes me."

"Have you decided what to do next?"

"Beyond talking to Della in the morning?" He shook his head. "I'll do that, find out exactly what drove her away from the warehouse, then I'll decide."

Perry asked the question she knew had to be asked,

the question that had been eating at her all night. "Does that mean you believe in her now?"

He didn't answer, and his hand stilled just long enough that Perry began to worry that he was thinking about leaving her alone in the bed.

But then his fingers began rubbing tight little circles on her hip, and his voice was dark when he said, "I'm not going to talk about it. About the reading. But, yeah. Whatever she can tell me about seeing Eckhardt? I'll pay attention."

JACK WOKE feeling beat instead of rested. Beat and cramped and uncomfortable, due to more than the bed. He was uncomfortable with the situation—being here with Perry and her aunt being upstairs, and her aunt knowing a lot more than he wanted anyone to know about his past.

It had been an off-the-books operation, an undercover assignment to infiltrate a human trafficking ring moving laborers from rural Thailand to L.A. He'd been taken on as a crew member on the cargo ship, and assigned to the galley, peeling potatoes, washing dishes, carting loaves of bread and buckets of broth to the men chained in the hold.

They had no clue that once they reached their destination they'd be working eighteen-hour days and have their contact with the outside world restricted. That they'd be subjected to slave-like labor conditions, held by induced indebtedness, and suffer non-payment of wages and the threat of deportation.

And what he'd done—freeing the men who'd been

unaware they'd sold their souls to the devil when they'd paid for illegal transport to the States—had pretty much been the mission's end.

It had pretty much been the end of his military career as well. Part of him regretted that it had gone down the way it had. But he'd considered his options, and found the good of the few to outweigh the good of the many.

Obviously, his superiors hadn't agreed. When his choices came down to desk work or a discharge, he'd whipped out a quick "*Hasta la vista,* baby," and gone into business for himself.

That business had now brought him Perry Brazille, and he was at his wit's end. What the hell was he supposed to do when his work took him everywhere, and he had no idea when he'd get back to New Orleans? He didn't even know her middle name.

He lay on his back, one arm hooked beneath his head, the other hooked around Perry where she'd backed up to him and was using his biceps for a pillow.

He wanted to wake her up slowly, to make love to her while she was still half asleep. No more of this power banging to rid himself of demons. He wanted to take his time with her, to learn and explore and enjoy.

But it was too late for any of that this morning, because in the next second he saw the light from the kitchen beaming down the hall and heard running water. Della filling the coffeemaker, he figured, easing out of the bed and slipping into his clothes.

He left his shoes for later and padded toward the

only aroma guaranteed to get him moving. He found Della standing in the open back doorway, staring out at the rising sun.

He shivered, but he didn't say anything. Instead, he reached up into the cabinet for two mugs and set them next to the pot. Then he crossed his arms and leaned against the edge of the counter, waiting for whatever she'd been saving up to say.

And since he'd expected something of the sort, her words didn't surprise him. "I never was much of a parent to Perry," she began. "I'm much too self-involved to take care of anything but myself. So realize that this is as disconcerting for me to ask as it is for you to hear, but what are your intentions toward my niece?"

He wasn't sure what to say. The question was so traditional, and Della was anything but. Still, with the way she was staring toward the courtyard fountain...

Jack felt his face heat. "Honestly? I don't know."

"And it's absolutely none of my business." Della sighed. "I'm sorry. It's just that Perry is all I have and I don't want to see her hurt."

Which made her a pretty good parent in his book. "I don't want to hurt her. I'm just not sure these circumstances are the best for starting up anything with anyone."

She turned from the doorway and faced him. "You don't believe in trial by fire?"

What was he supposed to say to that? "I believe it happens. I don't believe it's always a healthy situation."

"You don't believe strong relationships can be forged under trying conditions?"

He didn't want to be having this conversation. Not when the subject of last night's reading was sure to come up, and Perry would be waking any minute.

And so he said, "Is that how it happened with you and Franklin? The murder and break-in and all?"

She smiled, the emotion more personal than a response to what he'd said. Except then she surprised him by saying, "Yes. And because of our circumstances, my circumstances, I've been afraid to believe."

He shook his head. "I'll never get that. How you can believe in things that can't be explained, but not in things staring you in the face."

"When it comes to looking inside ourselves, blindness seems to be more common than insight."

She closed the back door and came toward him, pouring the coffee into both cups. He sipped, she sipped, neither of them speaking further of the last several hours, the truth of what had passed between them a strangely solid bond.

Moments later, Della set her cup on the counter. "He's drowning, Jack. I don't know if he's literally in water, or if he's ill, but he can't breathe. He's gasping and struggling."

Jack's pulse exploded. "Eckhardt?"

"Yes."

"You tell this to Franklin?"

She nodded. "I called Book when I got up to my room last night. I saw orange. Rust or mud, I can't be sure. It could have been dried blood." She shook her head, let it droop on her shoulders. "Or it could be that drowning was how he died."

"Then what about the warehouse? What you saw there? The way it hit you? If he was already dead—"

"I don't know, Jack. I just don't know." Della reached over, wrapped her fingers around his wrist and squeezed. "What I do know is that this is where you take what I've given you and run."

And that would mean doing it his way, the feds, the NOPD and Detective Book Franklin be damned.

A BROKEN HEART. She'd never known how the shattered shards could cut like the blade of a knife. Her two men, they were so very different. And she loved each so very very much.

Drake was an artist. A sensitive soul who knew life was best lived in bright colors, that chances not taken were fortunes not made. She talked with him about dreams and desires.

Bruiser was a protector. A man of authority who understood black and white, right and wrong. She talked with him about wanting new curtains for the bedroom.

She slept with them both. Sang to them both. And when she loved one, she never considered she was betraying the other. She was the only one naive enough not to see the truth.

For the truth was that all Drake wanted was his music. He was moody, and he took to drink. He often forgot that she was in the same room, or even that she was in the same bed.

And Bruiser wanted respect. He wielded his power

as a knight of old wielded a lance, a Greek god a lightning bolt. She'd felt the sting of both.

She couldn't live with the one man. She couldn't give up the other. Her only choice was to start over. To make a new life on her own. If she fell in love again, then she would know this decision was the one she'd had to make.

Bags packed, she looked over her shoulder one last time. She even blew a kiss at the room she'd loved so much. Smiling, she turned to go...tripping over the vase Bruiser had bought her, Drake's flowers falling with her as she tumbled down the stairs.

13

Groaning, Perry climbed onto the stool behind the counter in Sugar Blues, swearing she would never be able to walk right again. Who knew that thirty daily—if rather lazy—minutes on the treadmill wasn't enough to keep her thigh muscles in shape?

Her next round of celibacy was definitely going to include a whole lot of leg lifts and cycling. Of course, she would prefer sleeping with Jack to sleeping alone, but she wasn't just anyone's fool.

He could stay in New Orleans for her, but why would he? He had a life, a career that took him places, one that didn't involve inventory and stocking and customer satisfaction, not to mention spreadsheets so accurately detailed, grown accountants wept with joy.

And really, she loved what she did. Her complaints weren't so much complaints as they were a comparison between his life of following leads left by kidnappers and hers, of filing. His background of shivs and bullets and traveling the world, and hers, of being unable to stick out four years for a degree at Loyola.

Not that she had anyone to blame but herself, if she was going to be dishing it out. She'd chosen the safety of this life, the comfort of the familiar, her own version of hearth and home and live-in ghost.

Yet after the sheltered life she'd lived, how could she have anticipated meeting a man like Jack? A man so utterly unique that she'd found herself falling for him in a matter of hours, falling into bed with him in a matter of days?

She couldn't have known. She couldn't have guessed. She was still reeling that it had happened.

When she'd finally woken this morning, he'd been long gone, the sun had long been up and Della had been standing at the foot of the utility room's bed with a cup of coffee for who knew how long. Not one of Perry's finer moments, in the face of the woman who'd raised her.

But Della had stayed, and they'd talked, they'd bonded, they'd shared an honest heart-to-heart about Perry's life. About Della's life. About choices they'd both made. About Book. About Jack. Mostly about Jack, though nothing about the midnight reading.

By the time Perry had climbed from bed, made her way upstairs for a shower and a change of clothes, all she'd wanted was to see him. Last night had not been an easy one, this morning equally troubled. They needed to talk. But he was gone, and she had work to do.

Della's first appointment was scheduled for ten. So when the bell on the door chimed fifteen minutes later, Perry glanced up expecting to see Mrs. Nielsen. The woman walking through the door, however—her designer heels clicking on the hardwood floor—was no one Perry knew.

A younger woman wearing baggy black jeans and a tight black turtleneck, her hair an unnatural red, followed. She stopped to browse the bookshelves, while the first woman headed straight to the counter at the rear of the shop, flashing a business card the moment she arrived.

"My name is Dawn Taylor. I'm a reporter with the *Times-Picayune*. I was wondering if you might be Della Brazille, and if I might ask you a few questions."

Perry took in the platinum-blond hair, the platinum watchband, the diamond teardrop in a platinum setting resting in the hollow of her improbably smooth throat. This woman was not the grieving widow of whom Perry had drawn a mental picture. This woman was anything but.

Her heart racing, her mouth dry, Perry glanced over her shoulder toward the beaded curtain covering the entrance to the hallway, then quickly looked back. The reporter already had her pencil and notebook in hand.

"No. I'm not Della. But I can schedule you an appointment to see her." Swallowing hard, Perry reached for the plumed pen.

Dawn Taylor's gaze flickered in the same direction Perry's had before returning to her face. She tapped her pencil to her paper. "Would you be her niece then? Perry? Perry Brazille? I understand her niece works for her. I don't see other employees…"

She looked away, glancing around the shop as if wondering how a business so small kept from going under. It was all Perry could do to stop herself from whipping out the shop's tax return.

"I manage Sugar Blues, yes," she said, sitting straighter. "But I don't know how I can help you unless you'd like me to show you around the shop."

Dawn shook off Perry's offer. "One of my sources tells me that your aunt was at the old Eckton warehouse yesterday before the site was raided."

"Raided?" Perry arched a brow, praying it hid the tic she felt at her temple. "I didn't know one could raid an empty building."

The other woman reached into her bag for a second pencil when the lead broke on the first. "Were you also there, then?" she asked, blinking rapidly. "Since you're aware of the building being empty?"

Shoot. Was it not common knowledge? Or had she just screwed up? "Everyone knows the building is empty."

"I doubt everyone has reason to know any such thing," Dawn Taylor said, jotting notes, her cell phone ringing before Perry could respond.

"Excuse me." The woman—a girl, really—who'd come in behind the reporter, dropped a text on sun signs on the counter. "I can't find a price on this book."

Perry grabbed two incense burners before they rolled to the floor. "If there's not a price on the spine, there should be one penciled inside the cover. See? Nineteen ninety-five."

She darted a quick glance at Dawn Taylor, who'd turned to take her call, then said to the girl, "Would you like me to ring that up for you?"

"No. That's okay. I'll come back for it. I didn't bring enough money."

"I'll keep it for you here at the counter until the end of the day," Perry said, but the young woman was already out the door.

Taylor clipped her phone shut to end the call and returned her notebook and pencil along with the cell to her purse. "I have an interview that's been bumped up in my schedule. I've got to go, but I will be back for your story, Ms. Brazille."

"I'll be waiting with bells on," Perry muttered under her breath, watching the reporter breeze out of the shop. She took a deep breath, wondering what the hell that had been about, and if she'd really messed things up, then slid the astrology book under the counter.

The bell hadn't finished its closing chime before Jack pulled the door open and came barreling down the center of the shop toward her. "What was Dawn Taylor doing here? What did she want?"

First things first. "Listen. If I'd had your cell number, I would've called you the minute she told me who she was."

He grabbed a crystal from the counter, rubbed it with his thumb. "Did she question you? Or talk to Della?"

Perry shook her head, returned her gaze from the crystal he held to his face. "She asked what I knew about the warehouse discovery yesterday. I told her to talk to my literary agent since I'll be selling the story, and that she'd have to make an appointment to see Della."

"Where is she now? Where's Della?" he asked, ignoring her sarcasm and bouncing the crystal in his palm.

"She must be in the kitchen, why?" she asked, glancing toward the door at the sound of the entrance chime.

Book came charging toward them, his face drawn. "Where's Della?"

Frowning now, Perry pointed over her shoulder. "In the kitchen."

He was around the corner and through the beaded curtain before she finished speaking.

"What's going on, Jack?"

"With him? I don't know. But Della told me this morning that she saw Eckhardt drowning. Guess what one thing never clicked?" he asked, his eyes sparkling, his excitement nearly palpable.

She, unfortunately, had absolutely no idea what he was talking about. "What?"

"Taylor. He killed himself by jumping from the Causeway Bridge. But it wasn't the fall that killed him. I pulled the information this morning. Coroner's report said it was death by—"

"Drowning," she said, finally catching on.

"Exactly. What if what Della was seeing was Taylor instead of Eckhardt?" he asked, lobbing the crystal to her over the counter. "It's way too much of a coincidence that both men drowned—"

"She's not in the kitchen," Book barked out, the curtain swinging in a wild tangle of beads behind him. "She's not in the utility room or in the courtyard."

Perry got up from the stool, a flitter of worry tickling her spine. "I've been here all morning. I would have seen her go upstairs."

"I'll check," the detective said, already climbing.

"The reading room, maybe?" Jack asked, heading toward the corner of the shop. "Did she have an appointment booked?"

"Yes, but the client never showed up, and the rest of her morning is clear," Perry said, grabbing the appointment book and scanning the page. "We had breakfast, then I showered and changed upstairs. When I came back down, she was finishing up the dishes. I've been out here ever since. I would have seen her if she'd gone upstairs."

She glanced up at the sound of Book's voice calling Della's name. As he came thundering back down the stairs, Perry's throat began to burn.

And she could hardly find her voice to ask Jack, "What's going on?"

He shook his head, scrubbed a hand through his hair. "Dawn Taylor is involved. She's gotta be."

"Dawn Taylor? The widow? What about her?" Book demanded.

"She was just here," Perry whispered, her eyes beginning to water, her chest growing tight. "She was looking for Della."

And now Della was gone.

"Perry. Walk me through exactly what happened," Book said, digging through his suit pockets. "Everything you can remember."

She started slowly, mentally retracing the morning's steps. "I was behind the counter. I'd just climbed onto the stool and was thinking about a conversation Della and I had earlier. I heard the chime and looked up, and that's when Dawn Taylor came in." Blew in. Like a hurricane. "She obviously wasn't here to shop because she marched right up to the counter and asked me if I was Della."

Book finally came up with a pen and notebook. "Did she tell you what she wanted with Della?"

Perry thought back, nodded. "She introduced herself first, then asked if I was Della because she had a few questions for me."

"Then what?"

"When I told her she could make an appointment, she asked if I was me. She knew I worked here. I told her I didn't see how I could help, but that I'd be happy to show her around the shop." Perry stopped, pushed her hair back off her forehead. "That was when she said a source told her that Della had been at the warehouse before yesterday's raid."

Book bit off a string of foul words. "Who the hell is talking to this woman? Where is she getting her information?"

Jack looked from Book back to Perry. "What did you tell her then?"

"I told her I didn't know you could raid an empty building, and she asked how I knew it was empty." She shrugged sheepishly. "I thought it would be obvious. I didn't even think."

"Don't worry about that now," Book said. "What else?"

Eyes closed, Perry rubbed at her temples. "She broke her pencil. Her cell phone rang. While she took the call, another younger woman brought a book up to the counter to check on the price. I told her what it was. She left, and then Dawn Taylor left, saying she had an interview."

Book scribbled a line of notes. "Tell me about the other woman."

"She was about twenty with bright red hair. Wearing dark jeans, a dark turtleneck and sneakers. She was looking at a book on sun signs."

"Did she buy it?"

"No. She said she didn't have enough money with her. I told her I'd hold it for her until we closed for the day."

"Did she say she'd be back?"

"Uh, no. She just left."

"Where's the book now?" Book asked.

Perry glanced beneath the counter. "It's right here."

"You don't think…" Jack started to say, letting the sentence trail off.

She looked from one man to the other. "Think what?"

"She may have been a diversion. Dawn Taylor came in and steamrolled you," Book said, and then he began to pace, gesturing with one hand as he talked. "The phone call could have been a signal."

"You're saying Dawn Taylor could be behind the Eckhardt kidnapping? And that maybe she's taken Della to keep her quiet? But why? Della doesn't know anything."

"If Taylor's not behind it, then she's being fed information from someone following the case—"

"Or from someone involved," Jack finished for him.

"So what are you going to do?" Perry wasn't even sure who she was asking.

"The book. The one the woman didn't buy."

Perry reached for it, and stopped when the detective held up a hand. And then she broke the bad news. "If you're thinking about her prints, you won't find any. She had on mittens."

"Mittens?"

Perry nodded, shrugged. "It's cold outside."

"I'm calling in a unit to go over the kitchen," Book said, grabbing his phone from the holster at his waist. "Lock up the shop. Don't let anyone else in, and you two stay out of the kitchen as well. I'll get a unit out here ASAP. And a patrol car to check up and down the block, find out what anyone may have seen."

"What about her walking stick?" Perry asked.

Book frowned. "What about it?"

"She's had it with her ever since getting her foot stitched."

The detective ran both hands down his face. "Damn. It's on the kitchen table. I just saw it. I didn't even think."

Perry swallowed hard, fought back tears. "What do you want me to do?"

"You stay by the phone. I'll make the calls and secure the kitchen," Book said, already halfway there. "And then I'll be at the *Times-Picayune* offices."

Perry turned to Jack. "Does he really expect me just to sit by the phone?"

But Jack didn't answer because now he was the one pacing.

"Jack! What am I supposed to do?"

He stopped, looked back up. "You do what Book says."

"And you?"

"I figure while he's at the newspaper, I'll pay a visit to the Taylor home."

BOOK LEANED against Della's kitchen door, his hands on either side of the new window, bearing his weight. Her walking stick lay on the table behind him—a big fat reminder of the support she'd provided him with the last two years.

He thought back to yesterday morning, to their time in bed before she'd had him find the stick in the attic. He knew she'd been trying to help, to make him feel better.

He just didn't see how anyone could understand the guilt he lived with when he didn't understand it himself. Then again, he hadn't given her a chance.

Of all people, Della would be the one to see the pent up emotion and the history behind what he'd stored. But now she wasn't here.

He'd been harsher than he'd meant to be, when all she'd been was concerned. Yeah, he knew he put in too many hours. Thing was, it was never enough.

Didn't the fact that she wasn't here prove it?

He'd brought her home this morning, after her visions during the warehouse visit had proved to be too much. He'd made sure Kachina would be around until Perry returned. All of that, and Della still wasn't safe.

He hadn't been able to keep her safe when that was

the one thing he knew how to do. Was trained to do. And yet, his experience didn't mean diddly.

She'd been snatched out of her own kitchen with her niece not fifty feet away, and a brand-new door between her and the world.

He didn't even want to think what she was going through. As strong as she was, she was still so fragile. So sensitive to the world around her.

He knew she was a survivor.

He just didn't know if she'd come home the same woman she'd been when she'd left. That frightened him, because that woman was the woman he loved.

And he didn't know what he'd do without her.

14

AFTER DIGGING furiously through papers stashed in his computer case like so much loose change—a mess Becca would kill him for making—Jack located Dawn Taylor's home address in his notes.

He couldn't remember when or where he'd found it, or why he'd written it down. He was just damn glad that he had.

His GPS navigator mapped out the drive, leaving him free to work at making sense of everything that had happened in the last two days. The fact that Eckhardt had been held at the warehouse—and recently—was indisputable, as was Della's vision of the severed finger before Perry had even found the damn thing.

What he was having trouble reconciling, however, was Della believing Eckhardt to be dead, then believing him to be drowning. And since nothing about her way of looking at things was scientific, there wasn't much he could do with the information but file it away.

If he'd been anywhere else, he might have started searching bodies of water. But New Orleans sat smack in the Mississippi delta, way too close to where the mouth of the river said hello to the Gulf of Mexico. And then there were the area's lakes and bayous and swamps…a needle in a haystack would be easier to find.

Most of all, however, he couldn't figure out what the kidnappers expected to gain by grabbing Della—except for the obvious. They'd taken Della to keep her from revealing to the police her visions about Dayton Eckhardt and his whereabouts. And damned if that wasn't eating at Perry.

Perry had barely been able to talk to the officers who'd responded to Franklin's call. And Jack hadn't been able to hang around for support. He'd wanted to be there for her; it killed him to leave. But he'd had this one window of opportunity to act.

He was supposed to stay out of the way, to mind his own business.

Like he could. Like he would. Time was still on Della's side, and Jack wasn't about to waste a second more than he already had.

He circled the block before parking two houses down and across the street. The neighborhood wasn't what he'd expected, and the house certainly wasn't one he would've imagined belonging to a reporter and a warehouse foreman.

Then again, the posh modern house could easily have been widow's spoils. Or a kidnapper's booty. Except that there hadn't been a demand made or paid out. Cindy had filled him in when he'd talked to her earlier today. She'd been glad to get the update, to see that he'd been busy.

Yeah, he'd been busy…cleaning up broken glass, replacing and painting doors, sitting for a psychic reading, falling for the psychic's niece and losing himself in her body. Not exactly how he was supposed to be earning his per diem.

To be fair, he had spent time in interviews, researching newspaper archives, following what leads he'd managed to turn up. Right now, however, none of that seemed like enough. If he'd done enough, he wouldn't be in the middle of breaking and entering and putting his PI license on the line.

It was almost as if he was losing his edge…

He'd knocked at the front door, watched for movement at the neighboring houses, checked the garage windows and a couple that were hidden by high growing hedges before making his way to the back of the house.

The door nearest the driveway opened into a utility room that opened into the kitchen. He found nothing on any of the entrances indicating an alarm, but he still planned to get in and get out quick like a bunny.

Problem here was, he had no idea what he was looking for. It wasn't like he expected to walk into the dining room and find Dayton Eckhardt digging into a bowl of gumbo.

Or to find a war board set up in Dawn Taylor's den outlining each step of the kidnapping plans. Though he wouldn't mind discovering a series of arrows on the floor, pointing his way to the end of the maze.

The biggest challenge to digging up clues was deciding what was a clue and what wasn't. The obvious didn't always pan out, even while those were the easiest onto which he could hook his trailer. Yet it was the tidbits of what seemed like useless minutia that often held the keys to opening the biggest doors.

But when he took his first step into the kitchen, he slammed to a halt, all thoughts of clues and minutia sailing right out the window of his mind. Della sat blindfolded at the eating nook table, her hands bound to the frame of the white garden chair.

She frowned and tilted her head to one side, listening as if knowing someone unexpected had arrived. He started to speak, to let her know he was there, but didn't have time. A twenty-something punk slacker stepped out of the pantry and back into the room.

"Dude." He dropped the box of Raisin Bran he held. He dropped his jaw as well. "What the hell are you doing here? No one's supposed to be here."

He was a scrawny pup, wearing black slip-on Vans, baggy khaki-colored jeans and a white logo T-shirt over a long-sleeved striped one. A black skullcap sat snugged low over his ears, causing the ends of his hair to stick out from beneath like so much dry straw.

He wasn't wearing anything over his face, which meant any second he was going to snap to the fact he'd just been made. And if there hadn't been a Browning automatic stuck barrel-down in his waistband, Jack wouldn't have hesitated asking him the same.

"Just doing my job," he finally said, and when he did, Della smiled.

"What the hell is your job? Who the hell are you?"

Obviously a brighter bulb than you, kid. Might be

a good idea to get the players straight in whatever game you're playing. Jack opened his mouth to answer, to talk the kid out of his gun and his hostage, but Della stopped him.

"He's the one who holds your fate in his hands."

Her voice came from that low, calm and soothing, but totally spooky place, the one she'd reached into when she'd spoken during Jack's reading. And he could see trepidation in the kid's eyes.

"Yeah, sure," the slacker boy sneered, gesturing with the gun he'd tugged from his pants. "You. Sit. And tell me what the hell you're doing here."

"I'm here for her," Jack said, glancing at the eating nook's cushioned bench, then pulling out a second chair from under the table. "What else?"

"How did you know she was here?" He'd moved to stand behind Della, his free hand gripping the lattice back of her chair.

Jack's gaze followed the slow rise of Della's chin, the cock of her head to the side as if she was taking measure of her captor and how close he was to the edge.

And then she said, "He's the one who found the finger. He's the one who brought me to the warehouse."

"Nuh-uh. I don't believe it. Kel said…shit." The kid looked ready to bite off his tongue. "I was told it was the other way around, you see. That you've been the one seeing…stuff."

A lackey. That's all this kid was. Left to stand guard over a female psychic half his size, twice his age and with a bandaged foot to boot—a thought that had Jack wondering what the boy would do if he realized how easily Della could reduce a grown man to a sniveling idiot.

Then he wondered how to get her to do just that, to see if between them they could get Slacker Boy to hightail it out of here in a panic, and lead them to the rest of the crew and to Eckhardt.

But it seemed she was one step ahead of him—else she'd picked the idea straight out of his brain—because she said, "All I can see is that you're wrong about the reasons Kelly left you here."

The kid shook his head, stared down at the top of Della's, his gun hand hanging at his side, his trigger finger twitching too much for Jack's comfort. "She left me here because she knew I could keep you out of the way while she and Pauly and Chris finished up with…shit. Shut up. Just shut up."

Dim, dim, dim, and about to sputter right out. Whoever Kelly was, Jack mused, Slacker Boy here was definitely her weakest link. And though he wasn't exactly thrilled with the way the kid's gun hand was wiggling like a worm on hot concrete, Della wasn't deterred by his orders.

She twisted on the seat, trying to face him. "It's not about keeping me out of the way. It's about not wanting you around anymore."

The kid was shaking his head. "Nuh-uh. What're you saying?"

Della took a deep breath, blew it out slowly, let her head fall forward in a slow, bouncing nod. "Kelly wants to be with Chris now. They're loading his Jeep to leave. She's done with you. She's set it up so Mrs. Taylor thinks her house has been burglarized. So she's going to be showing up here soon, with the police, who will discover you here holding me."

Slacker Boy shook his head, his eyes wide as he waved the gun around. "I don't believe you. Kelly wouldn't do that to me. She said they'll swing by and get me and leave you tied up here. Kelly said no one will believe Taylor when she says she has nothing to do with all this. That she didn't arrange it all for revenge. If the psychic's here, tied up so she can't shoot her mouth off to the police about where Eckhardt is, until it's too late for that dude. Shit. Just stop talking already."

Jack had no idea how much of what Della was telling the kid was true, but it was working. He backed across the kitchen, his soles squeaking on the floor, and placed the gun on the kitchen counter to pull a Sidekick unit from his pocket and frantically type out a message with his thumbs.

"I wouldn't send that if I were you," Jack said, hoping it wasn't too late.

"And why not?" the kid shot back, still typing, not even looking up. "Kelly will prove the psychic's wrong."

"What if she proves that she's right?"

He stopped typing, one thumb shaking over the keypad. "How's she going to do that?"

"Say Kelly doesn't answer." Jack nodded toward the messaging unit in the boy's hands, gauging his chances of getting to the gun before the kid snapped. "You've just let her know that you're onto her. You've given her and Chris time to skip out and dump on you and Pauly."

Slacker Boy stared at what he'd typed for several seconds, then turned and stared out the window that faced Taylor's side garden. "This is all so bogus. Kelly's been with me since eighth grade. She only met Chris when we were working at Eckton."

Eckton. Glory freakin' hallelujah. The connection Jack had been looking for. This kid and his cronies knew the man, knew the company. Had no doubt been caught up in the layoffs, same as Bob Taylor. But instead of jumping off the closest bridge, they'd cooked up their own special payback for their ex-boss.

Jack would give the kid a couple of minutes. Let him mull over his choices. Wait for him to figure out that his cohorts were the ones in the driver's seat, that he'd been left behind and was about to be roadkill.

Once he got that far, then it would be time to explain that saving his own hide meant making a deal—and he'd do it while working to part the kid from his gun.

"You know that it's genuine," Della said softly, and even Jack glanced over at hearing that voice that chilled blood. "You were wondering about Kelly and Chris long before all of you lost your jobs. They started coming in to work earlier than you. You saw them sitting close in the employee cafeteria. The nights when you left early and Kelly stayed, Chris stayed, too. You know that. And in your heart, you know they weren't working."

Jack waited, watched the kid squirm, the color drain from his face, the soft echo of Della's voice settling like a friendly noose around his neck.

"That bastard." Slacker Boy tossed the messaging unit across the countertop and picked up the gun. "He swore they were just friends. I am so going to rip his face off."

He paced the width of the kitchen, his long gangly arms swinging, his shoes screeching on the floor. And then he stopped and said to Jack, "Get up. Untie her. We're outta here."

"All of us?" Jack asked cautiously, pushing to his feet.

"Yeah. What, you think I'm going to leave you here to rat me out to the cops?"

"You can't get out of here with both of us," Jack said, working at Della's bonds. "Two against one?"

The kid snorted. "Two against me and the Browning, you mean."

Jack indicated Della with a nod. "She's blindfolded. She hasn't seen you. Can't I.D. you. So just take me. Leave her here. She's not a threat."

"I don't know that. She pretty much seems to know everything about Chris and Kel."

Sweat broke out on Jack's nape. "She doesn't know half of what I do."

The kid looked over, his eyes wide and red. "What do you think you know?"

"She can tell you what's going on with your people." *Steady, ol' boy. Steady*.

"Bullshit."

The kid appeared more bewildered than ever. And so Jack pressed. "You don't need both of us, dude. You take on two more hostages, you're really screwing with your odds of making it out of this thing in one piece. Not to mention screwing things up even worse with Kelly."

"All right, all right. The psychic stays here. Stand in front of her and let her tie your hands. And leave the blindfold on, lady. But first, you—" he started jerking open kitchen drawers, finding an apron and tossing it to Jack "—tie this around your eyes."

Jack took the apron and folded it into a long thick strip, slipping his keys from his pocket into Della's hand when he turned. She squeezed his fingers in understanding, and once he was trussed to Slacker Boy's satisfaction, he let the kid guide him toward the door.

"You, lady. Keep the blindfold on and don't move until we're out of the garage and gone. Wait thirty minutes. I swear, if I see a single cop before then, your hero here gets a bullet in the head."

PERRY SAT at the table in her aunt's kitchen, her head down on her crossed arms. She couldn't bring herself to move. She didn't think she could answer another single question. She would, of course, if anyone could come up with anything new and useful to ask.

But the repetition and circles weren't getting them any closer to locating Della or finding out who took her and why. She hadn't heard from Jack since he'd left to check out Dawn Taylor's house, and since he still hadn't given her his cell number, Perry couldn't call.

Book had returned and was talking to the federal agents who'd arrived twenty minutes ago. His visit to the *Times-Picayune* offices had turned up the reporter in the middle of the interview she'd claimed to have scheduled when she'd flown out of Sugar Blues earlier in the day.

Her visit this morning was now looking more like an elaborate setup in which she hadn't been aware she was playing a part. She was willing to go to jail to protect the name of the informant who'd pointed her in Della's direction, but why she'd been pointed that way, she hadn't a clue.

Her own history with Eckhardt was simple enough. After her husband's layoff and subsequent suicide, she'd sued the firm for the couple's emotional distress. She'd never expected to win the case.

The gesture had been all about making a statement—or so she'd said to Detective Franklin. She'd wanted to go public with details of the way the Eckton employees in New Orleans had been left high and dry when Eckhardt had pulled up his Big Easy roots.

Book, however, had learned the whole story after wrangling a few legal strings—that having the money to do so and preferring to salvage what remained of Eckton's good name, Eckhardt had silenced her with a settlement. And, as part of the agreement, had the court records sealed.

Dawn Taylor would want for nothing the rest of her life. Didn't say much about her convictions, Perry mused. But then, seeing the reporter this morning, it didn't take a big stretch of her imagination to picture the woman finding comfort in all that cash.

Unfortunately, they were back to a big fat square one, and Jack was out wasting his time. He needed to be here. She needed him here. She needed to feel his arms around her, to absorb his strength.

She needed to lean on him while he reminded her that as small and fragile as Della appeared, she was nothing of the kind. She was strong. She could make it through anything. And Perry knew he was right—as long as anything didn't include whoever had her deciding she was too much of a threat to keep around.

Seconds after the thought crossed her mind, she heard a vehicle drive up and a door slam in the alley. She glanced out the open back door and saw Jack's SUV. Relief surged through her.

She got to her feet in a whirlwind, shouts rising outside, and Book looking out the kitchen window behind her saying, "Della."

He ran out with Perry on his heels. Della had only made it halfway to the fountain before they reached her. And then their questions fell one on top of the other. "What happened? How did you get free? Who took you? What're you doing with Jack's keys? Where's Jack?"

All Della could do was shake her head. Swearing under his breath, Book finally swept her up in his arms and headed for the kitchen, calling over his shoulder for an officer to radio for a medic.

Perry rushed to keep up, holding her aunt's hand until they reached the door. Once inside, Book set Della in one of the chairs while Perry hovered, feeling useless, finally putting on water for tea.

Book didn't even give the federal agents a chance to get close. He knelt in front of Della, holding both of her hands in his, his voice breaking when he asked, "Are you all right?"

She nodded. "I'm fine. But you need to find Jack."

Perry caught back a sharp choking sound, as Book asked, "What's Montgomery got to do with this?"

"He found me. At the reporter's house. They were holding me there."

"Dawn Taylor's?"

Della took a deep breath and nodded again. "The group behind Eckhardt's kidnapping are trying to set her up as the one responsible."

Book snorted. "They're not doing a very good job. We just cleared her."

"Wait." Perry placed her aunt's cup of tea on the table. Liquid sloshed over the side. "What about Jack? Where is he?"

"I don't know, Perry. I'm sorry." Della held out a hand. "I haven't been able to see anything yet. I had to get back here, and there's still too much noise, too much energy. I can't focus."

"Let's take this one step at a time," Book said, boosting up from his knee and pulling a chair close to face Della's. "Anything you know, anything you learned. We need to know."

"I didn't learn anything. Not until Jack arrived and the man holding me started to talk." She twisted her fingers together. "I say man, but he's so much of a child."

"A child?" Perry asked, moving to a third chair and

leaning into the table, her arms outstretched on top as she reached toward her aunt. "What do you mean, a child. How old?"

"Early twenties I imagine. But he seemed to be no more than a teen. There are four of them. They worked at Eckton Computing. Chris, Kelly, Pauly." She closed her eyes for a moment, her hands wrapped around her teacup. "And I believe this one's name was Kevin."

Book's pen scratched across his notepad. "They have Eckhardt—"

"And Jack," Perry put in, flexing her fingers and trying not to claw a hole through the table. "Eckhardt and Jack."

"Right." More notes. "Is Eckhardt—"

"Alive? Yes. But that's all I can tell you. I don't know where they're holding him."

"What about the kid who took you?"

"Very thin. Six feet tall. Blue eyes. A narrow face. Blond hair that's a bit long. He wore a knit ski cap, so it was hard to tell, but at least over his ears."

"What was he driving?" Book asked, his pen flying.

"A very small foreign car. It was white, two doors with a hatch in the back. And a logo of some sort across the rear window." She paused a moment, then said, "A surfboard. Or perhaps a skateboard. I can't see it clearly."

"Did he have a weapon?"

She nodded. "A handgun, yes. He held it on me while I tied a scarf around my head as a blindfold."

Perry could see the color rise on Book's face as he made his notes. It hit her then how very much he cared for her aunt, how anxious he must have been waiting for news on Della.

The way Perry was anxious now, knowing nothing of what had happened to Jack.

"What happens now?" she asked, fearing the answer, waiting to hear that Eckhardt came first—after all, weren't the federal agents here for him?—and that Jack was a back burner item.

"The medic will check Della over," Book said, silencing Della's protests before she did more than open her mouth. "We hit Eckton's personnel files, connect one of the four to the car Della described, put out an APB—"

The ringing of the phone cut him off. Perry glanced over, glanced back. Della hadn't been gone long enough for tracing equipment to be put on the line. "Do you want me to answer that?"

Book nodded solemnly, got to his feet. Perry did the same and crossed to the counter where the handset sat cradled in its base. She took a deep breath and picked it up, her heart in her throat as she said, "Hello?"

Both Book's and Della's anxious faces looked on as she waited, expecting the muffled or distorted voice of Jack's kidnapper making demands.

But all she heard was background noise. The sort that usually meant a cell phone had mistakenly—and randomly—dialed a number from the bottom of a pocket or a purse.

Book listened in, waited, then shrugged. She hung up, wishing not for the first time that Della had caller ID. "There's no one there."

"Do a call back," Book said. "Star sixty-nine. See what you get."

She picked up the phone, frowned when she heard no dial tone, pressed the receiver down and tried again. Nothing. She shook her head, held out the handset. "I can't get a dial tone. Whoever called is still connected."

15

SLACKER BOY may have been a few fries short of a Happy Meal, but the rest of the crew was prime Kobe beef. Jack felt like he'd been shuffled straight from the steam table into the Sorbonne.

His only saving grace was that they hadn't yet discovered his cell phone in his pants. Then again, if the connection had timed out before anyone figured out who was calling, his goose was undoubtedly cooked. So much for all his intensive, specialized training.

After he'd blindfolded himself and Della had tied his hands behind him, Slacker Boy had stuffed Jack in the back floorboard of a tiny import and covered him with a tarp. And stuffed had been the truth of it. The car was the size of a lunchbox, and Jack was a full course meal.

He'd tried not to breathe in the mold spores and cat hair, or more than one layer of the dirt ground into the carpet, and had managed to tuck his chin to his chest and use his sweatshirt as an air filter—not that the fabric had done much to help with the smell.

He'd also managed to twist his hips in one direction, his arms in the other, and grab his cell phone off his belt. It had taken a furious amount of concentration to not only remember Della's number, but to blindly dial it when he was facedown on his knees and the keypad was upended behind him.

But he finally did, slapping himself a mental high five when he heard Perry's muffled greeting. He'd then pushed the phone into his boxers and prayed that when Slacker Boy stopped the car, he could shake it down his pant leg to the ground and kick it out of sight.

Not that it would've been easy, being blindfolded and all, but he'd never had the chance. The minute he'd been hauled to his feet, he'd been hauled away from the car. He'd listened closely before being pushed up what he thought were porch steps, trying to pick up exterior noises, but heard nothing he could identify.

No traffic, no voices, nothing except what sounded like tree frogs, lapping water and rustling leaves. And that made a whole lot of sense considering everything around him smelled wet. The air was heavy with moisture. The ground squished beneath his feet. He smelled compost and fish and weeds. And the pungent bite of cypress.

Drowning. This was it. What Della had seen. If he didn't figure out where he was, if the cell phone call didn't lead Franklin to this location…Jack didn't even want to think of what Eckhardt had suffered because he was pretty damn sure he'd be suffering the same.

He needed to know where he was. What he did know was that he'd ridden on his knees with his ass in the air for not quite an hour. He'd counted off the minutes until his legs had gone to sleep. He'd spent the rest of the ride trying to keep his head off the floor.

Not knowing the area and not being good on directions with his internal compass bounced all to shit, he wasn't going to be a whole lot of help letting anyone know where he was if he got the chance. But he was pretty damn sure he was in the middle of a swamp.

He stumbled over the threshold when Slacker Boy pushed him across the porch and through the door. And then he was met with scrabbling feet, a lot of foul language and a loud female screech.

"Kevin, you moron!"

Kevin had hold of Jack's elbow and jerked him to a stop. The shrill voice probably belonged to the love of Slacker Boy's life, Jack mused.

"Where's the psychic? And who the hell is this?" Same voice. More attitude.

"He's the one who knew about the finger and about Eckhardt choking. She didn't know any of that. She told me you and Chris were running out on me and Pauly."

Kevin rattled it off in such a hurry, Jack could almost hear the kid sweat.

"And you believed her?" Shrill became a shrew.

"Yeah, and you know why, Kelly?" Kevin's voice rose to an ear-piercing decibel. "Because she knew about you coming back to the office when Chris worked late."

"God, Kevin, can you freakin' forget about Chris for a minute?"

Jack turned his head to the side, heard footsteps pacing a hardwood floor. The shrew went on.

"So help me, if you've screwed this whole thing up

because you're jealous of Chris, I will never let you climb into my bed again, got it?"

"What the hell's going on, Kel?" This was another male voice, deep, beefy sounding.

Kel blew out a heavy breath. "Kevin decided not to stick with the plan. He let the psychic go and brought us this guy."

"Who is this guy?" Beefy Boy asked.

"Someone who seems to know more than he should," Kelly said, the tone of her voice not exactly music to Jack's ears since she'd gone from shrill to sinister. "Take him out back and tie him up. Tie him good, got it? Wait. Give me his wallet."

Kevin dug into Jack's pocket for his wallet, ran across the bulge of his cell phone on the way out. "What the hey? He's got a wire or something in his pants."

"Sheesh. Unbelievable. Just unbelievable." Kelly was obviously not too happy with her man. "Where?" she asked, and seconds later Jack felt her cool fingers diving into his boxers. "It's his cell phone, you moron. You brought him out here and left him holding his phone?"

"He was tied up, Kel. It's not like he could make a call."

"It looks like he did just that." She paused, and Jack heard the snap of his phone closing, listened to her rustling through the papers in his wallet. "Oh, isn't this just rich. He's a private dick. From Texas."

And then Jack felt her up in his face. "What about it, dick? You working for that bitch, Cindy Eckhardt?"

"Sorry. My client list is confidential."

It was when she shoved the barrel of a gun into his throat that he first got nervous. And it was when she whipped off his blindfold and got up in his face that he finally began to sweat. "Answer me."

He weighed Cindy's right to privacy against his right to live and tell his grandchildren about this adventure. He looked down at the girl who was no bigger than Perry and said, "The Eckhardt family hired me, yes."

"What have you told them about us?"

Where Perry was gypsy wild and gypsy hot, Kelly was a throwback to bad Goth with thick black liner ringing her eyes and burgundy black lipstick painting her lips. Layers of long-sleeved T-shirts clung to her body. She'd tucked the tops into the jeans that hung low where she should've had hips. A wide belt studded with eyelets served to hold up her pants and holster the gun she carried. And this hideout was nothing but a fishing camp. "Nothing. I don't know anything about you."

"How'd you find Kevin then?"

"Because I went looking for Dawn Taylor." Jack was beginning to wonder if the laws of deduction applied only to him. "That was the direction you were pointing the authorities."

"Kel?" Kevin's question barely drew Kelly's attention. She did no more than bark out a sharp, "What?" before pacing the width of the tiny room.

There wasn't much to see here, but Jack took it all in. A brown Naugahyde sofa, a matching club chair, the material of both cracked and peeling and stained.

The floor was the same planking as the walls. One door led off the main room toward what looked to be sleeping quarters—two walls lined with bunks.

And then all that was left was the kitchen—no more than a hot plate, a sink, a small refrigerator, and all of it powered by what sounded like a generator running out back. Folding chairs sat grouped around a card table. Empty chip bags and candy wrappers and soda cans sat on top.

"You weren't coming back for me, were you?" Kevin was saying, trying to get Kelly's attention and getting Beefy Boy's instead.

The bigger man stepped into Kevin's space. "Leave her alone. Let's figure out what we're gonna do now."

"Get out of my face, Chris," Kevin snarled, and headed toward the back room.

O-kay, Jack thought, wondering how this bunch had managed to do anything right when it seemed the only thing they had in common was getting into Kelly's pants. He shook off the thought, got back to thinking about the long shot of getting the hell out of here.

It wasn't being in the middle of nowhere that had his gut tied in a knot. It was being in the middle of a bunch of armed lunatics with a big fat morale problem and a bucket of life sentences hanging over their heads that had him just about ready to puke.

"Take the dick out back, Chris," she finally said. "I'll figure this out."

Chris gave a laugh that curdled Jack's stomach even more. "How 'bout I send him out to Eckhardt. The guy could probably use the company."

"No, not yet. We have to wait for Pauly, and that'll give Kevin a chance to chill. Besides, I need time to think." She stopped pacing, rubbed at her temples and a moment later looked up.

Jack swallowed hard. The dark emptiness in her eyes was more malevolent than the gun in her hand, more deadly than the flat, lifeless tone to her voice when she said, "I need to decide what to do with this dick who just stepped up and ruined my life."

GREEN. Thick and ripe. Slithering. Deep. Verdant. Hues of grey and blue. Bottomless black.

Crushed bone between teeth. Talons tearing, shredding. Ropes. Everywhere ropes. And cold.

Life. A thread. Seeping strength. Seeping water. Wings. Fins. Scales. Fangs. Men.

Red. A heart beating. A heart slowing.

A heart stopped.

Rubbing her temple with one hand, Della took the stairs slowly, sliding her fingers along the brick wall wondering, as she had before, why Sugar stayed. If she had no choice. Or if she had found in death what she had missed in life. And, if that was the case, what it was.

Knowing that Perry waited anxiously with Book in the kitchen, Della slowed her steps even more. What the rest of the day brought to this household would change the future for many. What she didn't know was who would celebrate the highs, and who would mourn the lows.

These were the times when her gift took on the

guise of a curse. Nothing she had seen could possibly be of use in locating Dayton Eckhardt. Or, she feared, Jack. Admitting this to Perry felt like a failure. She knew her niece was looking for hope, and she had none to offer.

Neither could she present Book with leads to follow or clues to unravel. She'd thought by taking time to free her mind of the day's lingering anxiety, she might connect with Jack as she'd been able to do today in Dawn Taylor's kitchen. She'd even hoped that she might find remnants of Kevin's energy as he focused on getting to Kelly.

The only thing she was able to find was a vast release of emotion flowing from Book. She thought she had driven him away by reaching into a past he didn't want her to see. So to learn now of his affection, his tenderness, his passion was a pleasure almost too rich to bear.

But this wasn't the time to dwell on what was personal. So, schooling her features, she stepped through the beaded curtain and into the kitchen, stopping in the entrance as all heads turned her way. "I don't think I'm going to be able to be of any help. I've seen thriving life." She steepled her hands, offered the prayer to Perry along with a request for forgiveness. "But I've also seen death. I can't identify anything more than what appears to be wildlife and wetlands."

Perry turned away, hugged her arms across her middle and stared through the window out into the dark. Della sensed the waves of worry, the fear for Jack's well-being swirling like an undertow and sucking her niece down.

She wanted to go to her, to offer comfort, but she had none to give. And so she turned her attention to Book, who was nodding his head, scanning his notes.

"Believe it or not, this is good. This is good. The phone call that came in earlier tonight? It came from Montgomery's cell. The last tower that picked up the signal showed him on the Lafitte-LaRose Highway headed south."

Book flipped through the pages in his notebook. "Kelly Morgan's family owns several hundred acres down in the Barataria Swamp near Jean Lafitte. Been in the family for generations. I'd say we start there."

"HERE'S THE THING, dick," Kelly said, stepping out onto the back porch of a house that Jack had decided, during the last couple of hours of freezing his ass off, was a hideout par excellence, sitting as it did on the edge of a swamp. If nothing else, this much they'd done right.

He didn't like his odds of being discovered. And he sure as hell didn't like his odds of getting out of here alive. Pretty damn humiliating to make it out of Chechnya and the Sudan with a couple of bullet wounds, to spend a month in the hold of a cargo ship, crossing the Pacific three times while being held hostage by the trafficking ring before he'd escaped, given no light, little water, and even less food, only to succumb to some snotty kids in a swamp.

He was old. He was soft. He didn't like being either. And he missed Perry beyond belief. So much so that not telling her how he felt was going to be his life's biggest regret.

When the motley crew inside hadn't been bickering like a flock of biddies, and his own teeth hadn't been chattering loud enough to break glass, he'd heard a diesel pickup or two chugging in the distance. But that was it. He could've shot off a flare gun and still gone unnoticed unless he'd timed it just right.

They'd tied him up, but they needn't have bothered. It was the middle of the night. He had no idea where he was. And without more than a quarter moon to guide him, he wasn't about to step onto a road and over a bump that might end up having bone-crushing jaws.

He couldn't imagine what Eckhardt must be going through. While securing Jack to the frame of a folding metal chair, Beefy Chris had taken great pleasure in pointing out where Jack would be able to see the other man once the sun rose over the swamp.

And since his pleasure-taking had also extended to circulation-strangling knots, Jack couldn't help but wonder about the pain of Eckhardt's bonds, and whether or not he could see the house from where the gang had tied him to a cypress root and left him to rot.

Kelly let the screen door slam shut behind her, pulled the string on the overhead light. Jarred back to the present by both, Jack glanced over.

Kelly leaned her flat ass on the porch railing and crossed her arms. "Dayton Eckhardt owes a lot of money to me and the boys. Money he doesn't have to pay us, you know why?"

Because you didn't leave him with his wallet when you left him to die?

"Because when he tore the company out of our

backyard like a big bad weed, he cut loose everyone but management. That included those of us with the biggest stake in Eckton's new software. The one we developed. We. As in me and Chris and Pauly and Kevin."

And to think. I'd pegged you as director of human resources. Or maybe fashion.

"Eckton filed the legal crap, the trademarks or copyrights or patents. Whatever. So Eckton owns the system. Our system. It was our teamwork, our vision. And it's our work that within a year is going to turn that billionaire in Redmond, Washington into the last best thing."

I'm sure Mr. Gates is shaking in his Gucci's.

"And now we have nothing. No stock options. No income. No residuals. We have shit. Got it? So we figured it was payback time. Let Dayton Eckhardt learn what it is to not only have zero, but to be a zero."

That was when Jack finally opened his mouth. "This is revenge? That's it?"

"Revenge. Making a statement. Seeing the man suffer." She shrugged. "Take your pick."

"Suffering. That's the reason for the amputation?"

"Seemed like fun, you know, putting the righteous fear into the cops and the wifey. You saw Pauly's message in the warehouse, didn't you? We've got what we want. A long, painful goodbye for Mr. Eckhardt." She tucked her fingernails into her palm and studied them. "Only now we've got this big dick of a problem. Namely you. So do we leave you here? Or take you with us?"

"Guess that depends on where you're going to go,"

he said, recognizing that smart-mouthing this chick wasn't going to earn him any points but, hell on a pirogue, this was nothing but revenge?

She snorted, started picking at the polish on one of her nails. "Funny thing about that. If you'd asked me earlier today, I could've told you. Now I'm not so sure."

Jack dropped his head back and cackled. "Then Della was right. You and Chris were loading up the Jeep to skip out on poor Pauly and Kevin."

Kelly's gaze shot to his. "She told you that?"

He shook his head. "She told Kevin that."

"God, he's such a moron," she said, rolling her eyes.

"And what does that make you, seeing as how you've been with him since eighth grade?" Jack prodded, watching for any glint of emotion.

If he hadn't been watching, he would've missed the flash that came and was gone. "Right now, it makes me the one everyone wants. The one everyone's looking to for a decision."

"Heavy load for those shoulders of yours."

She shrugged. "You look smart enough to know that size doesn't matter," she said, and tapped a finger to her head. "It's all about what's up here."

"Then why don't you use what's up there and cut me loose." He jerked once at the ropes. "Eckhardt, too. If we're both good to go, then it's no harm, no foul. We all get up and have our Wheaties for breakfast."

"Puh-lease," she said, with a defeatist's sigh and a shake of her head. "It's Kevin who's the moron, remember. Not me. I'm not planning to spend time behind bars."

"You didn't think about that before you started this?" he asked.

"All I thought about was putting Eckhardt through some heavy-duty shit. Just like he did with us. Payback's a bitch, haven't you heard?"

"So, now what?"

"Actually, I was thinking of ending it all right here." She reached for the gun, shook her head, rubbed the mouth of the barrel along the side of her ear. A cold chill settled in to scrape at the pit of Jack's stomach. Morons this bunch might be, but stupid they were not.

"Okay, look. That's not going to solve anything. And you're smart enough to know deals are made all the time. Especially with a lot of juice to bring to the table. Which I'm pretty sure you have."

For several long seconds, she stared into Jack's eyes. Hers were lifeless, cold, flat. He worried that it was too late, that he'd waited too long to speak, that he should have tried to bond with her, shown empathy instead of sarcasm, let her see he was on her side— even though he wasn't—and talk her in off the ledge.

Except then, in the next breath, she doubled over and spit out a laugh, waving the gun like a flag. "You really thought I was serious, didn't you? Damn, am I good, or what? No wonder Kevin needed a psychic to tell him he's out of the picture. I still can't believe he couldn't figure out for himself why we left him at the reporter's house."

Jack closed his eyes, shook his head. Son of a flippin' bitch. He and the horse he'd rode in on were both screwed. The only deal this one would be interested in was a part in a teen slasher flick—as the slasher.

Biting down on a whole lot of words he knew he'd better not say, he looked back up. "What now?"

She took one long hop toward him, leaned down and flicked the end of his nose. "Tell ya what, dick. As soon as I find out, you'll be the first to know."

And then she yanked on the chain pull, leaving him in darkness as she walked out of his life.

16

"YOU KNOW I'm not going to handle it well if they don't find him," Perry said to Della. The two women were sitting together at the kitchen table, as they'd found themselves doing so often lately—and always, it seemed, in the middle of the night.

With Jack's kidnapping falling under local jurisdiction, Book and his partner hadn't given the federal agents on the Eckhardt case time or room to object, but had arranged to meet officers from the Jefferson Parish Sheriff's Office at the Morgan property near Jean Lafitte.

The feds had followed because, thanks to Jack, they'd been handed the closest thing to a clue they'd had in the Eckhardt case for days. Perry doubted she and Della would be handed anything before daylight.

That was assuming Jack was being held at the Morgan place, and the search parties picked the right place in all that swampland to start.

It was also assuming those in charge didn't decide Jack could wait, that Eckhardt was a priority. That first they needed to get to him.

"They'll find him." Della reached over and patted

Perry's hand, her fingers cool and smooth. "Book will find him. He knows Jack's one of the good ones. He won't leave him out there any more than he'd leave one of his men."

Perry could only pray Della was right. "I still can't believe what he did, charging out of here the minute we realized you were gone. I mean, I love what he did. I'm in awe of what he did. Losing you would be unbearable." She sighed, drooped against the table. "But he's only known us a few days. It just seems so…"

"Heroic?" Della supplied, a wise brow arched above her eyes, which shimmered a deep purple hue.

All Perry could do was nod because she couldn't think of a more perfect word. Jack. A hero. Her hero. Her eyes filled with tears. Her throat ached and burned. The last thing she wanted to do was cry, but her emotions wouldn't have it any other way.

"It's been an extraordinary few days, Perry," Della said softly as Perry sobbed. "And he's an extraordinary man, doing what men of his nature do. As is Book. They may try a woman's resolve, but they are men worth loving that much more because of who they are."

Perry swiped the back of her hand over her eyes and, desperately needing a distraction, considered her aunt. "You love him, don't you? You love Book. I've wondered for a long time, but it's all over your face."

Della pressed her fingers to her cheek, then reached for her teacup. She didn't try to hide any of her smile. "I certainly didn't mean it to be so obvious. I hope I didn't embarrass him."

"Embarrass Book Franklin?" Why did that make Perry want to laugh? "Is that even possible?"

"Of course it is." Della frowned. "What sort of question is that?"

Sighing again, Perry slouched back in her chair and crossed her arms. "I don't know. It's a man question. A species I know nothing about."

"And now whose feelings are written all over her face?" Della teased, lifting her cup to sip.

"I never believed this would happen." Perry closed her eyes, dropped her head back. It felt so heavy she wondered if she'd be able to lift it again. "And I don't just mean that it would never happen to me. I didn't think it happened at all."

"What, love at first sight?"

"Funny. And here I thought it was heartburn."

Della chuckled. "You haven't been exposed much to romance, Perry."

Oops. Not sure this was a conversation she wanted to have, she leaned forward and reached for her tea while changing the focus to Della. "What about you?"

"What about me?" Della hedged.

"Do you know why *you* haven't? And do you know how horrible I'm going to feel if it has anything to do with your responsibility to me?"

"Truthfully? You've always been a consideration, but never a burden," she hurried to add when Perry groaned. "You've always been a very welcome part of my life. Having you would never have kept me from a relationship if I'd found a man who could deal with my gift. I never did. I'm still not sure that I have."

"Book doesn't seem to have any problem dealing with it."

"The problem is more mine," Della said, her fingers growing white where she gripped her cup. "It's hard to respond only to what he wants me to know, and not to what I know he feels. There are times I'm not sure I can tell the difference. And it seems easier not to try."

"And so you're going to give up? Give *him* up?"

She dropped her gaze, smiled softly to herself. "You don't think I'm too old?"

"To do what? Live? Love?"

"To start over."

Perry suddenly felt like the wise, experienced one when she was nothing of the sort. "It's not about starting over, Della. It's about starting again. It's about change. Who said we have to pick where we live and how we make a living and who we let into our lives, and stick with that plan forever?"

"Good." Della's hand came down flat on the table so hard that her teacup rattled. "Because now that you've said it aloud, I'm going to hold you to it."

Sneaky woman. Perry narrowed her eyes. "We're talking about you and Book. Not about me and…whoever."

"You and Jack. And yes we are. Like I said. Extraordinary. The days. The man. The whole world out there waiting for you to embrace it. The only thing tying you to New Orleans is familiarity."

"You're here. Sugar Blues is here. This is my home. And…" She groaned as her own words came back to haunt her. "I'm in trouble, aren't I?"

"That's something only you can figure out. But what I know is that you're thirty years old, Perry. It's time for you to step outside your comfort zone and give life, and love, a chance."

JACK HAD NEVER given the prospect of dying much thought. Hell, he'd almost died of frostbite hunting down a group of Chechen rebels who'd blown up a school, killing over two hundred children. He'd almost expired from heatstroke rescuing aid workers captured by the Sudan People's Liberation Army. But all that was before he had Perry.

Now all he wanted was to get the hell up off the ground, and get back to Perry ASAP.

He had no idea how long he'd been lying alone in the dark in the dirt with a gash pouring blood from his head, but it was long enough that he was almost too stiff to move.

In the end, Kelly did nothing more to him than drive off and leave him to his fate there with Dayton. That was it. Did they freak out? Chicken out? He would've laughed if he'd had the energy.

He'd heard the engine of Kevin's car sputter twice before turning over, followed by the sound of what had to be Chris's Jeep. Ten minutes later, all that was left was silence. Ten minutes after that, what few night creatures didn't mind singing in the cold had started up.

Knowing it was going to be a hell of a long time until he saw the sun, he decided not to waste it. He hadn't taken but a quick look around while the light was on for Kelly's visit, but he had seen enough to know he and his chair were the only things on the porch. Meaning his best bet was to get off and find something—a broken bottle, a crushed can, a sharp edge on the generator, a gator's jaws—to cut through his ropes.

The one piece of metal he knew he could use if he broke it just right was his chair. Options weighed, he'd busted loose one section of railing with his shoulder, then rocked himself right off the porch.

He was out for a while. He didn't know how long, only that he came to feeling like an almost corpse. His head ached like a burst watermelon, his joints like seized gears, and his balls had never been so cold.

He flexed toes, then ankles, then knees, then hips, finding the lower half of his body working. His hands seemed okay, and he didn't seem to have dislocated either shoulder, or busted his elbows—a mean feat since his wrists were bound behind him.

But it wasn't until he rolled to his side and up onto his knees that he realized how badly bruised he was going to be in the morning.

And then the knees thing didn't seem like such a good plan at all because the chair on his back knocked him forward, and the ground came rushing up to meet his face. He lay there, hands sagging from the chair frame, and recovered his breath.

What a way to find out you were truly an ex in the special ops biz.

In the past, survival had been about getting back to his unit, getting hooked up with another operation, getting his ass back out in the field.

Now, surviving was about getting back to his woman. He would've laughed, but he already had enough dirt in his mouth as it was. Four days—five days?—and that was exactly how he thought of her. It had been a hell of a wake-up call to discover what he'd been missing.

He really didn't want to have to miss out on any more. And so he crunched his abs—his only muscles that didn't ache—and pulled himself up to sit on his knees, then made it all the way up to his feet. He swayed to one side, stumbled looking for his balance, but finally found it.

Walking with the monkey of a chair on his back and one eye caked shut with dried blood kept him on a pretty short leash. The hulk of the house loomed in shadow, and he headed toward it, catching his foot on a tree root and crashing to the ground with a rib-crushing oomph.

Hell on a crutch. He did not want to lay here like alligator bait until morning. He closed his eyes, screwed them tight, and concentrated on Della, hoping there was some psychic tide flowing out there in the ether, and that she could catch his wave.

Thirty seconds later he realized the sharp stabbing pain in his back wasn't a broken rib but a piece of the chair. Finally! His trip to the ground had busted the frame. He was lying on one hand, so he twisted the other, tugging until the rope slipped free from the broken end of the metal tubing.

He used his teeth to undo the knots at his wrist, then sat up and swung the rest of the chair around in front of him. By the time his other hand was free, he felt as if he'd mainlined adrenaline. He needed a lantern. A flashlight. A canoe or a raft, and a paddle.

And he was on his way to find them when he heard the first car. He felt like an island castaway, wanting to jump up and down and wave his arms. But he didn't. He hurt too much. And the headlights—two sets of them now, no three—were cutting through the trees.

So he leaned against the porch and waited, raising a hand to the level of his good eye and squinting into the glare. The first car threw up rooster tails of gravel and dirt as it screamed to a stop. The door slammed open. Book Franklin charged out.

"Montgomery!" he yelled.

Jack lifted his other hand in acknowledgment, saving his breath and waiting for the detective to get close. "You're looking for a Jeep and a Civic hatchback. Not sure on the Jeep, but the Civic's white. Early nineties."

But Book was already nodding. "We got 'em. We knew about the Honda. Had the plates. Two vehicles that close together, this time of night, on the Lafitte-LaRose Highway? We stopped them both."

Jack breathed a painful sigh of relief. "Della told you about the car?"

"She did. Where's Eckhardt?"

"I don't know exactly." He turned, pointed in the general direction. "That way, somewhere. I was just about to hunt down a raft and paddle out."

"You look like shit, Montgomery," Book said, clamping a hand down on Jack's shoulder. "You go wait in the car. We'll bring him in."

"He's got to be in bad shape after all this time."

"Yeah. I've already called for an ambulance."

"Good. Thanks."

"For what?" The detective smiled. "Doing my job?"

"Yeah," Jack said, shaking the other man's hand. "For that."

FINISHING UP everything he had to do took Book forever. He knew it was part of the job. He didn't mind that it was part of the job. He just wanted the job finished because he wanted to get to Della.

Protocol be damned, but he'd done the bulk of his interview with Jack while the investigator was having his head stitched up in the emergency room. Eckhardt was in surgery—finger aside, he and his heart were in fairly good shape. He had a broken ankle pinned and wouldn't be giving a statement anytime soon. Jack had given Book the number, and he'd called the wife in Texas. She was on her way.

The four kids who'd snatched the computer chief were in federal holding, making for one less task Book had to finish up tonight. Tomorrow would be a hell of a long day, one better tackled after food, sleep and making love to Della.

It was late afternoon by the time he dropped Jack at Sugar Blues to pick up his ride. Not that Jack had anywhere he needed to be—or anywhere Perry was going to let him go. The minute he climbed from the car, she was out the back door, running, screaming, launching herself into his arms.

Book walked right past the younger couple. He only

had eyes for the woman standing framed in the open back door. She was so beautiful, his Della, and damn if that wasn't exactly who she was. Exactly who she'd been since the night he'd first found her sitting on the courtyard fountain, drenched to her skin.

He stopped in front of her, looking up from the step that led into the kitchen. He was still an inch or two taller, but he liked seeing her at this level. They were almost face to face. And he didn't think he'd ever seen her eyes so dark purple.

Or so teary and red. "Are you crying?"

She nodded. "Of course, I am. Aren't you worth crying over?"

His heart fluttered, but he frowned anyway. "I wasn't the one in danger."

"You're always in danger." She reached for him, caressed his face with her fingers. "Every day that you go to work, you're in danger."

"I am who I am," he said with a shrug, her hand cool and soft and the only comfort he needed.

"I know that." She blinked. She smiled. "I wouldn't want you to be anyone else. I wouldn't love you if you were anyone else."

"Then you can live with that?" Damn voice, cracking like that. "Knowing there's always a chance when I leave that I might not come back?"

"I know it already." Her smile broke the dam holding his emotions. "I've lived with it every day for two years."

At the sound of doors slamming and an engine roaring to life, he glanced over his shoulder and watched Jack and Perry drive away. "He's a good guy. I wasn't so sure about him at first."

"That's because you saw too much of yourself in him."

He turned back, curious. "Am I really that cocky?"

"You can be."

"Hmm. I'll see about making a change."

"Don't you dare."

And if that didn't just make his heart—and other things—swell. "You like me the way I am, huh?"

"I love you the way you are."

The swelling went on. "Then is there any particular reason you haven't invited me in?"

"None that I can think of. As long as you're sure this is where you want to be."

When she said it, the brimming tears fell from her eyes, and he caught himself unable to speak. His throat clogged. His chest burned. He swore he was about to have a heart attack. And so he took her hand, smoothed his thumb over her fingers and brought them to his lips.

The kiss stopped time. It was a moment he'd never forget. She smelled of soft flowers and jasmine tea, and it was the scent he'd thought of for so long as belonging to him. The same scent he'd learned meant home.

He kept her hand in his and captured her gaze. "There is no place in the world that I'd rather be. No person in the world who means to me what you do. Della Brazille, I have loved you forever, and more than anything I want for you to be my wife."

"I'll marry you tomorrow, Book Franklin. I'll marry you today. If I could marry you this moment, it wouldn't be soon enough for me," she said, before she wrapped her arms around his neck and cried.

He held her, feeling his heart burst open in his chest, then finally smiled against her ear and asked, "So *now* do you think I can come in?"

She laughed, stepped away from the door and gave him the greatest privilege of all by letting him into her life.

17

"I WANT YOU to make love to me," Perry said, closing her townhouse's front door and leaning back against it. She'd spent all day waiting to get Jack alone.

Hours had passed between Book's phone call relaying news of the double rescue and his car finally turning into the alley behind Sugar Blues. Jack had climbed out aching and exhausted, his visit to the hospital behind him, more with the NOPD and the FBI to come.

She knew he was as tired mentally as physically, and she too was running on empty. But right now, she had to be with him. Nothing else mattered but feeling as if they were one.

"You do, do you?" Jack said, flopping down onto her couch and slouching back like he owned the place, legs spread wide, arms propped on the top of the plush cushions, eyes closed and head back.

"Yes. I do." She turned the lock. It caught with a loud click. "We're together and we're safe. We don't have anywhere we need to be for hours. And I don't want to do anything between now and then but enjoy you."

He opened his one good eye, the other hidden with a bandage, and glanced over. "I can't believe I'm saying this, but where do we need to be hours from now?"

"When it's time, I'll tell you." She pushed off the door, walked to where he was sitting, stood between his legs and held out her hand. "But right now all I care about is letting you know exactly how happy I am that you are alive and a part of my life."

He wrapped his fingers around hers and brought them to his mouth for a soft, lingering kiss before tugging her down and tumbling her across his lap. "I'm pretty happy that I'm still around to be here."

She didn't ever want to relive those hours of waiting to find out if she'd see him again. Watching Della get out of Jack's SUV had started a roller coaster of emotions. The up at finding her aunt unharmed. And then, the big lunge over the summit and down. Down, down, down.

She'd thought she would never stop falling at the news of Jack being gone, had wondered if she would ever be able to eat or breathe or sleep again. And then, realizing she'd hung up the phone on his call…if there had been another more panic-filled moment in her life, her memory had long since filed it out of reach.

Looking up now into his eyes, she realized how close she'd come to losing him—a realization that made her want to hold on to him forever, to hold on to him as hard as she could.

Without smothering him, of course. Or causing him to choke. Or making him feel as if she'd stolen his will and his freedom.

"Jack?"

"Perry?"

"Do you want to be here? With me?"

She asked the question softly, because suddenly she wasn't sure of the answer, and she had to know. They'd been through an unbelievable experience. And in so many ways, they were nothing alike.

She still didn't think he believed in Sugar, though Della was a different matter. Yet both were so much a part of Perry's existence it was hard to accept that her reality wasn't the same as Jack's.

But she would. Just as she would accept that he wouldn't talk to her about what had happened in his past. At least not yet. At least not for a while. And probably never about all of it.

He waited so long to answer, her fears grew to astronomical proportions. And she thought she would die when he finally came back with, "Do you want the truth?"

She nodded. She couldn't deal with anything less.

"No," he said, taking a deep breath.

"No?" she squeaked out. *Oh, no.* This was not what she wanted to happen. Not what she wanted to hear. She started to sit up.

He pushed her back down, shook his head. "No. This couch is way too small for the sort of night you're talking about. It's the bedroom, or you can forget it."

What a silly, silly man. How would she ever get enough of him? She looked down, smoothed her rumpled skirt. "Then I suppose we should just forget it."

He barked out a laugh. "As if that's going to happen."

And then she was the one laughing because he surged off the couch, swung her up in his arms and carried her to the bedroom as if she weighed no more than a pillow and he wasn't hurting from head to toe.

She wasn't about to spoil her caveman, hair-dragging fantasy by telling him he needed to put her down. Instead, she laced her fingers behind his neck and held on, loving the feel of his muscles flexing, his arms, his chest, even his abs that tightened as he walked.

She remembered the first day she'd seen him, the day he'd walked into Sugar Blues and approached the counter, all long legs and delicious motion. Closing her eyes and seeing him move while her body enjoyed the fruits of his long-legged labors, well, it just wasn't enough.

She wanted more. She wanted him all. And so she raised her head and nipped at his earlobe before whispering, "Hurry."

He chuckled. "Aren't you the one who just said we don't have to be anywhere for hours?"

"Yes, and I don't want to waste a minute between now and then," she said, barely getting it out before he came to a stop. She tilted her head back to meet his gaze. "What? Why aren't we moving here?"

"Close your eyes."

She did, but still she asked, "Why?"

"Close your mouth."

She did, and this time asked nothing.

"Now, I'm going to prove to you that we could stand here all night and we still wouldn't be wasting our time."

She knew that. Truly she did. But she was thirty years old, and she'd never expected to feel for anyone what she felt for Jack, and it just seemed as if they would run out of time before she got half her fill of having him.

His words, when he spoke, came out on a gruff whisper, a raspy sandpaper sound. "Did you know that with your arms around my neck like that I can feel your heart beating against my chest? That I can feel the curve of your breast?"

When she started to open her mouth, he leaned down and silenced her with a quick kiss. "I can feel the strength in your hands and your arms, and all I can think about is having you stroke me the way you did that morning in bed before I took you in the shower."

His voice was low, a heated vibration against her shoulder and the breast she pressed against him. Her nipples hardened, and her skin began to sing from the rush of blood just beneath. She thought about stroking him, about tasting him. She thought about taking him deep into her body.

Her impatience returned, and she murmured, "Jack."

He chuckled again, but he did start walking, pushing open the door of her bedroom with one foot, stopping once they'd made it inside. He lowered her slowly until her feet touched the floor, letting her body slide the length of his and holding her close all the while.

He moved his hands to her bottom and squeezed, pulling her belly to his. His thick erection throbbed between them, sending arousal twisting through her in a heady, burning rush. She stood on tiptoe, opened her mouth over his throat, and drew on his skin until he groaned.

But it wasn't enough. And as much as she understood that none of this was wasting time, she couldn't curb her impatience to have him naked above her, to open her legs and welcome his body into hers.

It was all about being alive and having him safe. It was a reminder of how empty her life had been before he'd walked through the door of Sugar Blues and filled her hours and days with the wonder of his company.

She grabbed the fabric of his T-shirt and tugged the hem from his jeans, sliding her hands up the bare skin of his back and soaking him in. He was warm and smooth, his muscles sculpted to the curve of her palms.

She walked her fingers the length of his spine, still kissing him there beneath his chin, rubbing her nose over his Adam's apple, lapping her tongue through the dip in his throat, until finally he joined her, rushing to remove the barriers of their clothes.

He jerked his way out of his shirt, tossed it to the floor, had her sweater over her head and off in a flash. She reached for the hooks of her bra. He pushed her hands away and did it himself.

Seconds passed and then she was as bare as he was. She pressed her breasts to his rib cage, her hands to his abs, her nose to the center of his chest. She nuzzled him there, breathed him in, worked her way side to side, blowing through his hair, searching out his nipples to kiss.

He held her by the shoulders, his chin up, his head back, the tendons in his neck straining. And he groaned when she tongued him, when she kneaded his pectorals with the motion of her chin. Her fingers drifted lower, popping the buttons of his fly one at a time.

He found the back zipper of her skirt and eased it down. She shimmied; her skirt fell. He stepped back and shucked off his jeans. She stood in her bikini panties. He stood in his Lone Star State boxers.

When she smiled and rolled her eyes, he scooped her up again and dumped her on the bed. She was laughing when she crab-crawled her way up to the pillows. He followed, and he wasn't laughing at all. He was so serious, his expression pained, and it frightened her.

She reached up with one hand, placed it against his cheek. "Jack? You're scaring me, here."

"I'm sorry," he said, shaking his head. "It just suddenly hit me that I love you."

She swore in that moment her heart stopped beating. She couldn't move. She couldn't breathe. She couldn't think. All she could do was whisper, "You do?" and when he nodded she burst into tears.

"Oh, that is so not fair," she sobbed, waving her fingers in front of her face, a stupid effort at keeping her eyes dry. "The man I love more than anything in the world says he feels the same, and I'm supposed to swoon. Not blubber."

"You're very cute when you blubber," Jack said, leaning down to kiss away her tears.

"I'm not. I'm horrible. I get splotchy and red-nosed."

"Then I guess it's a good thing it's dark and I can't see you, isn't it?"

And that, of course, made her giggle, and the sobs started up again, and she couldn't tell if she was laughing or crying, and whatever it was she couldn't stop. All she could do was throw her arms around his neck and hold him tight.

He put up with it for about a minute. After that, he pried her hands away and sat back to get her out of her panties. His boxers were the next to hit the floor, and then he lowered himself between her spread legs, hips to hips, chest to chest, mouth to mouth, and kissed her.

It was a kiss of two souls, a mating that happened with nothing but lips that came together, and eyes that met, held, and couldn't look away. It was a kiss that lifted her up, that showed her that the rest of her life was filled with possibilities.

And when she pulled up her knees and hooked her heels in the small of his back, he entered her, pushing deep and settling there. His mouth never left hers. He laced their fingers together and pressed their hands against the bed on either side of her head.

He consumed her. He possessed her. He became the only thing she knew. His body moved over hers, the slow in-and-out motion of his cock creating a wicked friction between her legs. She pulled her mouth from his, tossed her head to one side and moaned.

He drove harder, buried his face in the crook of her neck, sucked the skin there into his mouth and swirled his tongue over the bruise he drew. She flexed her hips, lifting to meet the rhythm of his strokes.

And then she turned back, seeking his mouth, sucking his tongue inside to mimic the mating of their bodies. It was a primal connection, a sweet sensation of hope, of sharing, of knowing this was only the beginning, of anticipating how far they had to go.

She loved him. Days and hours and minutes didn't matter. She loved him. And she told him so with her arms wrapped tightly around his shoulders, her legs tightly encircling his back.

He shoved forward, and she caught him, holding him to her heart as he came. She followed, breathing in his air, reveling in his release, losing herself in the spiraling emotion consuming her body and soul.

THE NEXT MORNING, JACK moaned and groaned his way into his jeans and the long-sleeved Henley T-shirt Perry had laid out before she'd stashed his duffel bag who knew where, and run out of the townhouse telling him to hurry.

He started to skip his shoes, but didn't want to end up running after her barefoot on icy sidewalks through Jackson Square, so he hopped from foot to foot as he pulled on his socks and his Reeboks.

He had no idea what she had up her clever little skirt; he might be wild and crazy about her, but he didn't always trust her any farther than he could throw her. Which wasn't far at all considering how easily— and how often—she squirmed out of his reach.

Still, he wasn't about to deny that he was amazingly,

incredibly, over the moon for her. He couldn't believe how one person—one little gypsy woman—could make such a profound difference in his life.

Yeah, he had a lot to go through to explain what had gone down with the case. And all that breaking and entering stuff meant he might end up losing his PI licenses. Plural.

But the good of the few was all that mattered in the end. Della was safe. Eckhardt was a mess, but he would recover. Detective Franklin had finally figured out his priorities. And Jack had done the same.

He stopped at the front door, finding a red envelope stuck to the door with a thumbtack. Frowning, he left the envelope hanging, pulling out the note she'd left him inside.

There once was a man from Nantucket…okay, from Texas. I've just always liked saying that. Anyway. This man had a thing for music, and a voice that could actually carry a tune. And if he's smart, this man, he'll bring his voice and meet me in the courtyard because I want to hear him sing.

God, what a woman, he mused, his chest so tight he ached with it. He had no idea what she was talking about; he couldn't care less. And he didn't even bother to lock the door when he pulled it shut behind him.

Perry was standing next to the fountain in the center of Court du Chaud, waving his sweatshirt like a flag and looking as if exploiting his weather weakness was her favorite pastime.

She turned a circle where she stood, her skirt flowing around her, her hair a cloud of corkscrew curls that were as soft as skeins of yarn. She laughed as she twirled, nearly losing her balance, stumbling back and catching herself against the edge of the fountain.

And he swore right then that he'd never had anything hit him so hard as his love for her. Right in the solar plexus. A big fat fist driving it home. She was exactly what he'd been needing to make his life complete. And wherever they went from here, he knew to expect a hell of a trip.

And then he heard it. Chasing Perry down the alley between the courtyard and Café Eros, he heard it.

The unbelievable sound of what had to be Heidi Malone—er, Heidi Tannen—wringing everything she could out of the Star Spangled Banner with her sax. Just like she'd done the day she'd walked into the band hall all those years before and blown him and the other guys right out of their shorts.

"Perry?" he asked, grabbing hold of her biceps, hauling her to a stop, backing her up against the alley's brick wall. "What have you been doing behind my back? And where the hell did you find the time?"

"What?" she asked, flipping her hair over her shoulders and fighting a losing battle with a smile. "You think a shop clerk who works for a psychic doesn't have it in her to do a little bit of private investigation on her own?"

A grin that felt like it belonged to the man in the moon brought up both corners of his mouth. "Are they all here?"

"Yep," she said, adding a great big nod. "And with

their significant others. Ben and Heidi drove over from Austin. Quentin came in from New York with his fiancée Shandi."

"And Randy?"

Her eyes widened. "That one you're not going to believe."

"After all we've gone through the last few days, and you still think I'm some doubting Thomas? Hit me, sister," he said, and hooked his arm around her neck. "I can believe anything."

"Okay. How about the fact that Randy's been living right here for about four months?"

"In New Orleans? You're kidding."

She shook her head. "Not just in New Orleans. Here. At Court du Chaud."

"Well," he said, feeling the press of emotion in the center of his chest. "There's only one thing to say to that."

"You love me?"

"I do love you." He leaned over, smacked her on the lips. "And it's going to take a while before I get tired of telling you so."

"You'd better not ever get tired," she said, and smacked him right back. "But what were you going to say?"

"Just the obvious."

"Which is?"

"That truth is always stranger than fiction."

SINGING THE BLUES for the rest of all time wasn't such a bad gig. The digs were okay, if a bit humdrum. And it would have been nice to reach a bigger audience, but at least the regulars were learning their lessons.

Mmm-mmm-mmm. So distinguished, that older man. So sophisticated. He would know about wine and about flowers. About the feel of nylons. And silk lingerie.

Ooh. The younger one, now, he was about all kinds of kissing. And, oh, the ways he could touch. Those hands. Those fingers. Made a woman weep with longing.

The dark-haired woman. Did she know how lucky she was? How much that man loved her. And her love for him was no little thing. It was big and beautiful.

A kindred spirit. A friend she wished she'd had back in the day. Such contentment. Such purely perfect peace. Sugar gave the older woman a wink. And the older woman winked back.

THE WHITE STAR
The quest continues with book #2 of The White Star continuity…

Jamie Wilson thinks his best friend, Marissa
Suarez, is dating the wrong men—his wanting
her for himself has *nothing* to do with his opinion.
When Marissa's apartment suddenly becomes
a target for thieves, Jamie steps up to the plate.
Maybe Marissa will finally see the hidden gem
he is—inside the bedroom and out!

Hidden Gems
by
CARRIE ALEXANDER

*Don't miss out…
this modern-day hunt is like no other!*